On a sheep farm in the Stormberg region of the North-Eastern Cape, novice biographer Jeremy Cranwell researches the life of a British general who fell from grace there during the Anglo-Boer War. Even in that rural fastness, however, the past proves no match for the present and Cranwell soon finds himself drawn into South Africa's conflict.

The central volume of an intended trilogy, *The Desecration of the Graves* is a powerful successor to the widely acclaimed *The Arrowing of the Cane*, winner of the prestigious 1988 Olive Schreiner Prize.

John Conyngham is a sub-editor on the *Natal Witness* newspaper in South Africa. He is married with two children.

BY THE SAME AUTHOR

THE ARROWING OF THE CANE

THE
DESECRATION
OF THE
GRAVES

JOHN CONYNGHAM

BLOOMSBURY

First published in Great Britain 1992

Copyright © 1990 by John Conyngham

This paperback edition published 1992

The moral right of the author has been asserted

Bloomsbury Publishing Ltd, 2 Soho Square, London W1V 5DE

A CIP catalogue record for this book
is available from the British Library

ISBN 0 7475 1120 9

10   9   8   7   6   5   4   3   2   1

Printed in Great Britain by Cox and Wyman Ltd, Reading

For Heather

'There are defeats more triumphant than victories'
— Michel de Montaigne, *Essays*.

PROLOGUE

At last it is finished. Three years of toil are over. Copies of that weighty sheaf on my study table (between the Zulu fertility doll and the shelf of obstetrical manuals) will to-morrow be winging their way to local publishers and others as far afield as London and New York. Like infant turtles fresh from the viscous security of buried eggs, many won't make it across the dangerously wide expanse of sand. The hurdles are too great. But at least one, I hope, will reach the scooting spread of the breakers and escape to a life of its own. Then, those three years will have been justified. Gatacre will have been resurrected and vindicated. He will, in a fashion, live again, his dignity restored.

The nobility of failure, that was my impetus. The notion that the heady rise to the zenith can be eclipsed by the after-math. Down, but not out, the victim can rally and continue, his actions ennobled by his silent acceptance of life after the fall. A proud stoicism has a strength of its own. And silence is imperative; there must be no whingeing. Just a gentlemanly tolerance of life's vicissitudes. In this my subject excelled.

In the southern distance a laden tanker appears around the headland from Durban, set for the East, with gulls wheeling in its wake. I take a beeline to it from the hammock beneath the bougainvillaeaed pergola, letting my gaze slip across the dunes and the jagged waterline of the surf. Several Indian fishermen are busy on the rocks, arcing spoons into the heaving blueness which periodically rushes at the buttress of a large rock pool, bursting up and over and into the shallow refuge among the red bait, sea anemones and fingerlings.

Gatacre: how the name's pronunciation matches the man. Gat-ikker, not Gat-acre. Harsh and staccato with none of the latter's softness. Tagged 'Back-acher' by his troops, he was lean and hungry, honed to a supreme hardness. Unfitness was anathema. What he could do, his men could do; that was that.

9

This premise, as we shall see later, was his Achilles heel. Men aren't automatons. Even seasoned troops will become mutinous or apathetic with extreme fatigue. There is always a breaking point.

Aromas from the kitchen announce that the crayfish we caught at dawn are being prepared by Katie for tonight's celebration. It won't be a big affair, just the two of us on the terrace with the sun withdrawing into the canefields and the sea thumping away beyond the dunes. She will, so she says, make a toast midway through our quiet revelry: turning to the study window she will wish the manuscript copies well on their long and arduous journeys; then, swivelling and facing the darkening slope of indigenous bush, appeal to any sylvan deities there for assistance. I, in turn, will thank her for appearing sylph-like during my tome's creation when, like Gatacre after Stormberg and Reddersburg, I was in despair. Crisp riesling will flow as we reminisce. And laughter, I hope, will compete with the sound of the sea.

The catalyst was a legacy from my father. A prominent Durban obstetrician, he was killed late one night while speeding to hospital for an emergency delivery. He was, found the inquest, responsible for his own death. Minutes before the accident, the mother was delivered of a stillborn child. Therefore, he died futilely in the line of duty. My bereft mother, unable to tolerate the too familiar surroundings of our house on the Berea, sold up and moved to her sister in Johannesburg. Inheriting this beach cottage and a sizeable slice of his share portfolio, I abandoned my medical studies and floundered briefly in business before taking the advice of some Eastern sage whose works I had been reading. Follow, he said, your *real* inclination. Freed from financial anxieties, I did just that, deciding to write a biography of Lieutenant-General Sir William Forbes Gatacre, one of that sorry squad of British generals whose careers were shattered by a combination of bad luck and carelessness during the Anglo-Boer War. Despite incredulity and accusations that the subject was too obscure to warrant a biography, I stuck to my guns. While Gatacre may not have been the archetypal tragic hero, he was a remarkable soldier, a self-made general at a time when nepotism was rife. After three years of immersion, I am now more certain than ever that his story is worth telling.

The scrunch of sandals on beach sand in the passage. Katie appears, declares that so far everything is ready for the celebration, and sets off down the slope with a screwdriver and bucket in search of mussels in the rock pools. In the year that we have been here together, she has taken to afternoon foragings on the beach and, recently, to pilgrimages to the towering dunes near the headland. There, crouched beside the sandy banks, she combs through the strata of shell fragments in a strandloper midden, excited by their antiquity, imagining the little people foraging, like her, among the pools. Then, climbing to the peak of the highest dune, she sits motionless on the sand, scanning the sea and willing herself to tranquillity. On those occasions when I have accompanied her, we have sometimes seen a school of dolphins and glimpsed their sleek forms slicing through the bellies of the waves. It is usually nearing dusk when she reappears on the terrace, her hair tousled by the wind or dangling wetly after a dip in the surf.

Gatacre was a Shropshire lad. Tradition has it that a family of knightly rank was granted a fief at Gatacre in the parish of Claverley at the time of the Norman Conquest and took its name from the place. My subject, William Forbes, the third of four sons and with an elder sister, was the twenty-second direct descendant of a certain Sir William de Gatacre in the twelfth century, himself descended from the Claverley Gatacres.

The house at Gatacre, during William's childhood, was a remote and wonderfully wild playground for the sons of a squire. This freedom and abundance of parental love resulted in the four boys growing up robust and with that confidence which stems from local prominence and deep roots established over numerous generations at a particular place. Of William's youthful exploits here is an example taken from the biographical apologia of him written by Beatrix, his second wife, several years after his death.

One snowy winter evening the three eldest boys set out to

shoot wood pigeons in the copses around the house. Wearing night-shirts over their clothes as camouflage in the white surroundings, they posted themselves in coverts some distance apart, waiting for the pigeons to return to roost. When the birds came winging through the fading light, William found himself well positioned and bagged forty-two. As they were more than he could carry, he bundled them up in his night-shirt and lugged them home. After depositing the birds, he alarmed his mother who, in the gathering darkness, was confronted by her son dripping with blood. A portrait of the soldier as a young man.

Away towards the dunes, Katie has stopped and is talking to the Indian fishermen, one of whose gestures are strangely disjointed. Like a character in an inferior animated cartoon, none of his movements is fluid. His rod, extended behind him, jerks anxiously. Suddenly he swivels, taking the strain, the line taut and the rod curved. Katie throws back her head, laughing. The fisherman, apparently laughing too, reels in, swaying from side to side with the effort.

The tanker is now directly out to sea and nearing the horizon. Set for that other world over the hill, as it were. From this vantage point, someone ignorant of the details of geography could be excused for believing that, with the watery crest reached, all is downhill to Singapore or Taipei, or wherever. But like so many things, it's all a matter of perspective: to others, we have horizons, and likewise they have to us. Conversely, until death perhaps, we cross no horizons of our own. Slowly, surely, that cargo of bulk sugar or whatever churns eastwards, hounding its own horizon.

Presently Katie appears over the brim of the terrace and crosses the lawn to the large umdoni with a shower nozzle suspended from it. Catching my attention through the study window, she points into the bucket and rolls her eyes in mock ecstasy. Turning on the tap, she takes off her costume and steps into the spray. The vigorous jet fans across her face and neck, rushing down her body, sluicing from her haunches and legs the sandy residue of her dune excavations. Months of beachcombing have transformed her into zones of cream and dull bronze. Flicking her hair back off her shoul-

12

ders, she settles on a wooden stool and massages her thighs into a rich lather. 'That Indian fisherman,' she calls through the spray, 'the small one with the bow legs, wants to talk to you.'

'What about?' I shout, moving to the open window.

'He wouldn't say. He just said that when he catches a big shad he'll bring it to you, and then you two can talk.'

'He probably wants a favour.'

'Why d'you think that?' she asks, soaping between her legs.

'The business about the shad. A gift is usually the method to soften you up first.'

She laughs, turns off the shower and walks to the verandah. 'Darling, please pass me that towel on the chair.' I pass it to her through the window as pools of water form around her feet, spreading across the tiles.

'It'll be a beautiful evening,' she says, turning towards the sea, her breasts tremoring in time with her towelling. 'Just right for the send-off.'

'Yes,' I reply, picturing us entering the bedroom many drinks later and entwining feverishly on the sheets before subsiding and lying moistly beneath the open shutters. 'Come here,' I beckon, and she leans through the window. We kiss gently and I caress her neck, my lips whispering across her skin as lightly as feathers.

'I'd better get dressed,' she says, a hand touching me gently, 'store it up for tonight.' As she walks naked along the verandah towards the front door, I watch her and delight in her beauty.

After Hopkirk's School, Eltham, London Gatacre continued to Sandhurst where he was undistinguished, leaving in December 1861 with the college 'Recommendation'. Commissioned as an ensign in the 77th Foot, he soon departed for India where he was to remain for most of the next thirty-five years. Service in the Sudan under Kitchener and divisional command in South Africa were still decades away.

I walk onto the terrace and, using binoculars, catch the coup de grâce: the small, bow-legged fisherman has backed up the beach, maintaining the strain, while his companions are gaffing the fish from the rocks. They are stumbling about in bursts of spray. One slips, then regains his footing. The fish emerges, flapping, and is dragged out of reach of the water. It looks huge: perhaps a barracuda or shark. The fishermen are granting it that respect demanded by razor teeth. Their antics are almost comical: clubbing it from a safe distance, craning forward, flailing, as the waves explode beyond them.

To study Gatacre's command in the Eastern Cape, and more specifically his defeat in the battle of Stormberg, I decided to spend a year on site, as it were, immersing myself in that region, researching. For a Natalian, accustomed to sub-tropical humidity and encircling luxuriance, the high still-ness and spaciousness of the Stormberg are another country. To feel the bite of those winters and the searing sunlight of those summers too is something foreign. Without a barrier of dense air to promote temperance, the thin clearness offers no resistance to the weather's whims, allowing an indulgence in extremes. At dusk the heat soon succumbs to chillness. At times, the humidity which I had cursed so often in Natal was something I hankered after. And yet there is a certain magic about that high hinterland with its wide plains and sudden koppies, its dusty roads and restless tumbleweeds. Sometimes, when I reminisce like this, I want to be back there, despite everything.

With *Dignity in Defeat*, my Gatacre biography, now finished and poised for departure, I am filled with that emptiness that so often follows a period of intense, con-centrated activity. Like someone bereaved (a complete manuscript is dead to its creator), I find myself drawn back to that year-long sojourn when the book was growing. Sur-rendering to this compulsion I will recount the period of my stay and some of the mechanics of the biography's creation. So what follows will be Jeremy Cranwell's account of the Stormberg, or a South African's account of South Africa.

But, of necessity, it cannot really be a spontaneous story. No account from the vantage of its completion can be totally honest. Recollections, being dependent on memory, never are. Also, there is the need for improvisation. Everything must be tempered by hindsight. And yet all is not lost; much is gained from this distant perspective. The essentials and the superfluous

14

can be separated. All the tedium, or that much which is unnecessary, can be excised, for it is selectivity that breathes life into a story. Without it, these pages would be an interminable succession of bland minutiae. Consequently, I will have to be ruthless, seeking only the corsetry that gives everything form. So here goes.

ONE

Heads impaled on a barbed-wire fence. That image domi-
nated my arrival at Skemerfontein. I had wound down from
Boesmansnek, crossed the wide plain and turned in at the
signboard with its merino ram illustration. On my right,
dividing the road and a field of turnips, were a line of cedars
and a fence. Only a clump of prickly pears intruded, almost
engulfing the remnants of a disused reservoir and briefly
interrupting the parade of trees. Otherwise the cedars formed
a towering escort up the gradual incline to the homestead.

Weary after my long journey and slightly apprehensive at
the prospect of meeting the Murrays, whose cottage I would
be renting for the following year, I drove slowly over the
drainage furrows and their accompanying humps, gazing
abstractedly at the flanking field and the straggle of poplars
beyond it. As I mounted each hump, so the fence lowered,
then rose again as I descended into the shallow furrow. It was
while I was thus bemused that the grisly display entered my
vision: four small heads with ruffs stiff with dried blood. As
I pressed slowly on, so I passed that gallery of dull stares.

When I entered the yard a Border collie bounded towards
me. Nimble and friendly, it gave my bakkie a cursory inspection — sniffing, cocking its leg — and then led me excitedly
across the lawn to a large stone house with a grape-vined
pergola over its patio. Visible through the front door's
stained-glass panels was a long passage with a hatstand and
tallboy, all of which became alternatively suffused in blue
and yellow as I peered through different panels. A clock
ticked somewhere inside. As there was no sound of footsteps,
I knocked. The raps resonated in the quietness. A windmill
nearby clanked and its rotating blades swivelled, nosing into
the light breeze. While the collie flushed a frog from behind a
gum boot, muffled sounds began to emerge from the passage.
A blur loomed behind the panels. The door opened and a

16

man emerged slowly.

Angus Murray was an elderly man with the slow, unruffled grace of a heron and the demeanour of someone deeply, and contentedly, introspective. His long, weathered face had that gentleness that exists in some people who have mulled at length over matters and accepted their conclusions; the peacefulness of someone at ease with his limitations. He appeared, in essence, monastic, in the nicest possible sense. 'Hello,' he said quietly, 'you must be Jeremy. Come in.' He gestured down the passage with a hand cupping the bowl of his unlit pipe, then accompanied me to the large sitting-room. 'Let's have some tea and then I'll take you up to the cottage.' Excusing himself, he disappeared briefly and I heard him speak to the maid in Afrikaans, asking her to make tea and to call 'the madam' from the garden. As he sat down, he removed a box of matches from his pocket and made as if to light his pipe, but didn't. Flies buzzed at the sash window.

'Ah yes, Gatacre,' he said quietly after we had exchanged pleasantries, 'what a strange, restless man ...' Then he stalled. I didn't respond immediately, hoping for more, but at that point his wife appeared. Although, to extend the avian metaphor, Mary Murray resembled a bunting, being compact beside her husband's leanness, she had a similar aura of tranquillity.

'Jeremy,' she said warmly, extending a hand, 'welcome.'

Tea arrived and our conversation flowed easily over the usual mundanities and tentative enquiries to a quietly animated discussion of the Anglo-Boer War in the Stormberg. 'The district,' said Angus Murray, 'was full of military activity. Troops and burghers were everywhere. We even had a skirmish. Up the sloot from those poplars.' He pointed. 'The British suffered six casualties. They're buried in a corner of our family cemetery near those tall cypresses.' He craned forward and pointed again. Through the window where the flies were buzzing, between streamers of vine which hung down from the pergola, I could see three dark pillars in the distance among the dry grass and a patch of khakibos.

The sun, disappearing behind Boesmanskop, fired the passage and sitting-room. Outside, towards the sheds, the shadows were lengthening and their lopsided replica of the pergola had reached my bakkie, banding its bonnet.

Then the image returned: those wizened heads on the wire; my mute welcoming party. 'What,' I enquired, 'were those animal heads that I saw stuck on the fence down the drive?'

'Porcupines,' said Mary Murray. 'Angus offers a reward for them.'

'Yes, they're a damn pest,' he said in his deliberate voice. 'They make an awful mess of the turnips. The kwedins kill them at night and leave the heads on the fence for me to count. They eat the meat. It's very good.'

Several cattle, followed by a herdboy, emerged from the cedars and plodded towards the sheds. Someone called from the dairy and the boy replied, slapping a cow on her rump, guiding her into the doorway. The long shadow beyond the silo was a dark corridor between the shearing shed and crush pen.

The sudden roar of the lighting plant and the gradual glow of the lights caused Angus Murray to stand up and intone, almost as if part of a mantra: 'It's getting on, we'd better be off, you mustn't be late.'

Armed with a food hamper from Mary Murray, and with Angus as guide, I drove slowly through the yard, over a cattle grid and onto a rutted track that led up the hillside from the homestead. As we climbed, so the valley opened below us: the house and outbuildings; the patchwork of lucerne and turnip fields; the sloot filled with poplars; and the veld beyond, with its clusters and straggles of sheep. Away in the distance, concealed behind clumps of trees, were, said Angus, the homes of neighbouring farmers. As I peered at the darkening plain, with the sun now merely a haze behind Boesmanskop, I remember thinking how sparse the signs of human habitation were beside the immensity of it all. Presently we reached the cottage on a shelf of the hillside behind the main homestead. Nestled against the foot of a cliff running along the summit, the simple stone building with its green corrugated-iron roof was backed by a crescent of pines whose sighing was, from that first moment onwards, the

18

dominant characteristic of the place. Only their incessant susurration seriously challenged the heavy silence. Other sounds were less persistent: the occasional clanking of the windmill behind the house as it shuttled on its axis; the soft rhythmical groaning of its blades as they gained momentum; and the resultant bright sound of the water as it gushed spasmodically from a pipe into the stone reservoir. Also transient were the warbling whistles of the starlings at their nests on the cliff; the cooing and fluttering of doves among the branches; and the sudden bleat of a sheep, seemingly free of the diminishing effects of distance, ringing crystal clear in the thin air. But always, poised like a wave, was the silence, eager to well up again.

Angus unlocked the door, turned on the gas and lit the lamps, and showed me the few rooms before declining my offer of a lift home and setting off briskly down the hillside. In the muted glow of the hissing lamps, I noted the sitting-room with its warm yellow-wood floorboards, large oak table and several faded armchairs. On the walls were watercolours of the surrounding countryside, painted by Angus's father, the cottage's last occupant. A reclusive naturalist, he had lived alone in those rooms for a decade before his death the previous year. Outside, I discovered later, were several other examples of his fey individuality: crude dolmens and circles of stones dotted about among the tussocks of dry grass on the hillside; devices, so I was told, by which he had mapped out his existence in harmony with his environment.

The sun was gone when I started lugging my baggage indoors, dumping my boxes of reference books on the sitting-room floor. After parking the bakkie under a lean-to beside the cottage, I moved through to the bathroom where, finding the water to be piping hot, I filled the cast-iron bath and spent half an hour luxuriating in it. Then I dressed and settled in a chair in the sitting-room, wolfing Mary Murray's sandwiches and drinking several lukewarm beers, opening them gingerly because of their volatility after the journey.

After the onset of mellowness, I became detachedly introspective and found myself marvelling that I was actually there: on an isolated sheep farm in the Stormberg in search of a long dead general who had, nearly a century before, fallen from grace among those hills. It seemed madness that on the death of my father I had abandoned my medical studies and the comfortable life their successful completion would have ensured to write the story of a forgotten soldier in whom few people, if any, still had some interest. However, I consoled myself that much of worth has its origin in some sort of irrationality. The proverbial reasonable man, for all his level-headedness, is seldom an innovator. Even if my biography failed, the very idea of it would have been a success. But, writing aside, the rewards I reaped during that sojourn were enormous. It was, without doubt, my watershed. In that brief year I learned more than centuries of conventionally respectable living could have provided. For this enlightenment I have both the region and my research to thank.

Taking Beatrix's biography to bed with me, I threw several blankets onto the patterned mattress and read by gaslight as the wind hushed the pines and the windmill clanked rhythmically. Then I turned off the light and lay in the darkness, listening to the then unfamiliar sounds outside and thinking with enthusiasm about the year ahead. But, as a touchstone, my eagerness wasn't unambiguous; being a night owl, my animation after dark makes even the greatest obstacles appear surmountable but at dawn they reappear in all their daunting reality.

TWO

On my second day at Skemerfontein the Murrays slaughtered a sheep. This means in South African parlance not that the Murrays themselves slit the animal's throat, but that they had a black employee of theirs do it for them.

I had strolled down the hillside to the yard where, after nosing through the sheds, I took a path behind a diesel bowser on my way to the cemetery. As I rounded a stone rondavel, I was confronted by two labourers with a struggling ewe. While one pinned down the animal's hindquarters, the other kneeled with an arm around its neck. On seeing me, both the men and the ewe froze momentarily and in that brief pause they resembled, I thought, two men and a woman petting. Or rather, because of their contrasting colours and positions, two dark men simultaneously enjoying the favours of a plump white woman. But then the ewe renewed her struggle, dismantling the tableau with a wild flurry of kicks, one hind leg breaking free from its constraints and thrusting a groove in the caked earth. Perhaps wanting to impress me with their deftness, the two men set to their task with grim efficiency. The animal's head was pulled back, exposing its white neck from the surrounding ruff of grubby wool. A penknife with a tartan plastic handle materialised and, with one sharp stroke, slit the throat to the bone. Blood spurted. And then it was over.

The men stood up and greeted me, and the slaughterer wiped blood from his knife onto the ewe's wool. I returned their greeting and made a lame comment in Afrikaans about a feast, at which they smiled wryly. As they began gutting the animal, making a deep incision along its belly to remove its entrails, I left and headed away from the buildings and towards the cypresses, where Angus the previous evening had said the cemetery was, in search of the graves of the British soldiers who were killed in the Skemerfontein skirmish.

I found the few tombstones in a stone enclosure. Among them were several Murray graves and from their dates I found Angus's parents and a younger sister who had died in infancy. The name Barkhuizen predominated, however, and I discovered later that they were a bywoner family who had been annihilated by the Black Flu of 1918—19. The entire family occupied one row of graves — from father and mother to the youngest child — with several relatives behind them.

The soldiers were in a block behind one of the cypresses: six mounds with a common obelisk. On the marble the inscription was admirably simple: 'In memory of six men of the First Battalion Royal Scots killed in a skirmish at Skemerfontein on March 4, 1900.' The names were then listed, five privates and a corporal, with 'For Queen and Country' in delicate italics at the bottom. Beside them, with a headstone of its own, was the grave of a Cape Policeman who had died after a riding accident nearby several months later.

The sight of that simple memorial to the soldiers was strangely moving. Like many others from the Anglo-Boer War, it was an unexceptional tribute to several probably unexceptional men and yet it had, for me, a strange nobility. Why, I didn't know. Was it because they were killed violently so far from home? Was it a romantic nostalgia for an Empire I'd never known? Or perhaps it was because they were Anglo-Saxon, like my origins, and their presence on that isolated farm provided some tenuous proof that I had a heritage in this country. They were my claim to belonging, notwithstanding their unpopularity with the present powers that be.

As I returned along the ridge to my cottage I could see far across the plain Angus Murray's bakkie circling a flock of milling sheep. With his head out of the window, Angus appeared to be looking for any sheep with soiled hindquarters. It is surprising how quickly the parasites gain hold — blowflies, eggs, maggots — until their rottenness proves fatal.

Like a tourist newly arrived in a foreign country, I spent my first few weeks at Skemerfontein immersing myself in my unfamiliar surroundings. Everything received scrutiny, for that was Gatacre's environment. It was those surroundings, or their prototype an hour's drive away, that had seen the proud martinet reduced to tears. Cities may be transformed in a decade but that dry, desolate landscape has a timelessness which permitted my re-enactments nearly a century after the event. Even the farm's topography seemed anxious to assist: the cliff behind my cottage, the hillside and the sweeping plain beyond the Murrays' house could, with a little imagination, be made the Stormberg battlefield itself.

During that time of acclimatisation, I divided my days into several specific periods. The mornings were spent in research and the afternoons on long walks, or expeditions to sites associated with Gatacre. At dusk I bathed, drank a beer on the verandah and then, with the onset of darkness, retired indoors to prepare my supper. At seven I listened to the radio news while eating my frugal meal and drinking my second beer. Two beers a day was a quota which I very seldom exceeded during that early period; later stresses, however, forced me to compromise. After supper and coffee I read the *Daily Herald* which the Murrays sent up to me when they were finished with it. In spite of the paper's parochialism, I enjoyed these sessions; there was something reassuring about the fetes and farmers' meetings, the bowls tournaments and stock sales. Here, I told myself, was an insular rural community peacefully preoccupied with sheep. Here were white Africans, far from the complexities of city life, who were at one with their environment. Drawing sustenance from the past, they would be ideally suited to my project. I was sure there must be elderly people whose parents had participated in Gatacre's downfall and who had stories to tell. I needed only to become integrated to find them.

On my return from the cemetery, I found an old black woman waiting outside my cottage. 'Good morning,' she said in Afrikaans. 'I want to work for you. It was I who heated your water last night and this morning.' And thus Hester Madala appeared. Twice daily for the ensuing year she stoked the fire beneath the forty-four gallon drum outside the bathroom and twice a week dusted and polished indoors. And so began a distant but wholly satisfactory relationship.

My work on the biography after my arrival at Skemerfontein was initially limited to intensive reading of primary and secondary sources on Gatacre's life, with emphasis on his command of the Third Infantry Division of the Army Corps in the Eastern Cape. Many of these books and documents I had brought with me, but others I had sent to Toomnek, the village which I visited weekly to buy provisions. While I had already completed most of my initial research, I needed to familiarise myself with the firsthand accounts written by local onlookers. It was they, after all, who had watched as the General advanced from Molteno only to return with his sorry force some fifteen hours later. These impressions were essential for they covered previously unchartered ground. If my biography was to succeed, it had to be different. It had to be more than a hack's hagiography and had to capture Gatacre's debacle at Stormberg and explain, by emphasising its peculiarities, why what was essentially a skirmish became the grim defeat which with Magersfontein and Colenso comprised Black Week and shocked the Empire.

Working completely alone is daunting for a young and inexperienced biographer. At times the sheer volume of information made assimilation and creation seem impossible. But when I began to falter, the Murrays, as if alerted telepathically, would invite me to supper and in their peaceful company many of my doubts would be dispelled. Angus, having lived his entire life in the district, provided crucial insights into that theatre of the war. Whenever I asked a question concerning Gatacre's strategy, he would answer after his usual pause, laying the issue to rest. Then Mary would offer a second helping and I would be sustained.

Initially, my afternoon walks were on Skemerfontein itself. Dressed in khakis and wearing velskoens, I walked up through the pines behind my cottage to a large cave with its few faded Bushman paintings: several matchstick men and a woman with bulbous buttocks. Then, moving along the contour, I found a steep, narrow defile between the boulders. On all fours, like the brave but hapless Royal Irish Rifles at Stormberg, I scrambled up over the grass tussocks and harpuisbos, emerging eventually on a shelf above the cave. Far below was my cottage and far below it was the Murrays' homestead. And across the plain were the flocks of sheep

24

whose pale shapes altered fluidly like protozoa under a microscope.

I then explored the wide, flat plateau which crowned an assortment of cliffs and steep hillsides. From this high, windswept grassland I had a vast view of the ochre plains and koppies stretching away into the distance. With only the occasional party of blue korhaans for company, and the even less frequent sighting of a grey rhebuck, I set out across the plateau, exploring it and mulling over my work as the sinking sun transformed the furtherest hills into a haze of ruddy serrations. On each outing I scouted a different part of the plateau, always extending my search until I eventually descended into a shallow basin beyond it. There, in a rocky gully which cleaved into a ravine almost devoid of vegetation, was a simple cottage with a windmill, shed, cattle kraal and several small fields of dry mealie stalks.

One hot afternoon, wanting a drink of water, I approached the buildings to find three men stalking a rocky outcrop. Craning forward, each held a shotgun at the ready as he advanced, stepping carefully with the slow, foot-rolling gait that one is taught in the army is the quietest. Alarmed, I was at first unsure whether to interrupt this strange manoeuvre, but just then the men seemed suddenly to lose interest in their quarry, turned, and, chatting animatedly, began walking back towards their cottage. It was only then that they saw me. Their expressions changed rapidly: from suspicion, to puzzlement, to delight.

Assuming them to be Afrikaans-speaking, I greeted them in that language and asked if I may please have some water. 'Yes, yes, certainly,' they replied enthusiastically, almost in unison, hurrying forward to shake my hand and introduce themselves: Koos, Naas and Oom Piet Roussouw: two middle-aged men and their elderly father.

'Come,' said Oom Piet with neighbourly warmth, grasping my sleeve and leading me to the cottage. Propping his shotgun against the wall of the voorkamer, he offered me a chair as Naas brought a jug of water and filled four glasses. Above us, among other photographs on the wall beside a deal dresser, was a framed portrait of former premier John Vorster; having come from nearby Jamestown, he was a local boy made good. After we had all drunk, they began bombarding me with questions: Was I the young fellow who was living on Murray's place? What was I doing there? Why was I walking alone on the hill? I answered systematically in my faltering Afrikaans, a little nonplussed at first by the barrage: Yes, I was the person; I was doing research for a book on General Gatacre and the Battle of Stormberg; I was walking on the hill because I wanted to get to know the area. After a brief pause and much nodding, they began another bombardment.

These interrogatory salvos, I soon realised, were in no way hostile but just the unreserved inquisitiveness of three simple people who had a surprise visitor. Especially a young Engelsman from distant Durban. When their initial enthusiasm had waned sufficiently for me to attack, so to speak, I asked them what they had been doing with the shotguns.

They laughed. 'Yes,' said Oom Piet with the mushing pronunciation of someone with few teeth, 'we were stalking a snake, a big rinkhals that lives in those rocks. For years we have been trying to shoot it but it is too clever. It bit a kaffir once but the doctor at Toomnek saved him. It also nearly bit Naas.'

'Its fangs hooked in my trousers. I hit it with a spade but it got away. There was poison running down my leg,' said Naas with a strange braying voice, pointing at his calf. It was only then that I realised that he wasn't quite right. His coordination was somewhat awry, resulting in his movements being strangely dramatic, as if the impulse generating them was snagged briefly before bursting through. And there was always a patina of saliva around his mouth. But his oddness had other manifestations, as I discovered several months later.

In line with my desire to glean as much historical information as possible, I asked them what they thought of Gatacre and the battle. It was Koos who answered: 'He was a good general but he was defeated because he attacked on the Sabbath. God punished him.' Of the three Roussouws, Koos was clearly the most erudite. His quiet response was particularly perceptive. Gatacre *had* planned his attack for a

Sunday in the hope that he would catch the devout Boers off-guard. The plan was sound but it was hampered by logistical snags. Gatacre's determination to keep on schedule for a Sunday dawn assault did contribute to its slip-shod execution.

As I returned across the plateau, with the sun descending behind Boesmanskop, I pondered the significance of Koos's observation. What, I wondered, were Gatacre's religious beliefs? If he acknowledged the existence of a god, he must have succumbed to pragmatics and subordinated his faith to sanction an assault on the Sabbath. On his defeat, and during the hours he spent agonising over it, the possibility of divine retribution must surely have presented itself. Had he, on the other hand, been an atheist, would he have dismissed the defeat as being merely due to incompetent guides and bad luck, or would he have been stirred into agnosticism by the realisation that he had defiled the Sabbath? It is an interesting conundrum. Some critics have asserted that Gatacre wasn't very intelligent; others that he was a two-dimensional soldier. But surely someone who responded so sensitively on occasions must have had some capacity for introspection. And after a post-mortem of his defeat, he must surely have acknowledged the possibility that it may have been God who'd punished him.

THREE

The village of Toomnek is little more than a cluster of buildings on the road between Boesmansnek and Queenstown. For most passing motorists it merely means several hundred metres at a reduced speed before they can accelerate again. Of all its buildings, the Dutch Reformed church is by far the biggest; only it is visible from any distance: an austere stone edifice with a towering steeple. Beside it along the main street are the usual enterprises of a platteland dorp, many of them hidden behind drab, peeling facades.

Approaching it from Boesmansnek, as I usually did, one passes first the two large Afrikaans churches and the smaller, sadder Anglican and Methodist chapels. Then come the garage and the Masonic lodge, followed by the Royal Hotel, butchery, bank, pharmacy and several trading stores which cater largely for a black clientele. Next, behind the rambling Co-op building and alongside the railway-line, is the large municipal cemetery with its small Jewish and Muslim sections — testimony to the few traders and their families who once played such an important role in the community before moving to the bigger centres or emigrating.

Three roads cross the main street at right angles, serving the untidy scattering of houses which have accumulated behind the shops. On the Molteno side these roads become rutted dirt tracks and meander into grassland, dwindling eventually into footpaths leading to the black township: a jumble of box-houses and shanties on the hillside above the village. An attempt by the whites to obscure the eyesore with a row of pines has failed; despite the maturity of the trees, the proliferation of shacks up the gradient has elevated a section of the township into visibility above the treetops. Every morning and evening, especially in winter, a pall of smoke from the hundreds of fires descends into the shallow basin, reminding the white villagers of its presence.

After my trips to the Co-op to buy provisions, I began to patronise the Royal Hotel's bar on certain evenings. My intention wasn't only professional: while I wanted, of course, to sound out the drinkers on the subject of Gatacre, I was also sufficiently lonely to need some conviviality. At about five o'clock on each occasion I sat myself at the bar and ordered a beer, making desultory conversation with the witless barman. A large, nervous man with an apparent need to exhale into beer glasses and to buff them vigorously, he wasn't good company, but he did introduce me to the regulars. The first to arrive were civil servants, mechanics and bank clerks employed in the village itself, but in hot pursuit came the farmers whose robust entry was often heralded by revving engines and the slamming of doors. Before long a momentum was established: an animated medley of bilingual conversation, laughter, and roars from the television set which presented a continuum of boxing videos.

Thanks to a camaraderie fostered by alcohol, I was soon accepted by the drinkers and benignly dubbed 'the writer from Murray's place'. Virtually all the locals had heard of Gatacre and knew the approximate location of the Stormberg battlefield. Several farmers had Anglo-Boer War graves and redoubts on their land. One farm, on which the General had bivouacked, was named Gatacre. A construction worker claimed that it was his grandfather, as a burgher in Commandant Swanepoel's commando, who was the first to see Gatacre's column from the heights of the Kissieberg on the fateful morning of December 11, 1899.

As was to be expected from a gathering so evenly divided between Afrikaners and English-speakers, views on the Anglo-Boer War differed widely.

With Afrikaner xenophobia and English jingoism forming the extremes, the middle ground comprised complex variations of compromises. No two views were identical. Some Afrikaners had the Anglophobia of their grandparents diluted by the marriage of English-speakers into the family. Several others with similar backgrounds had past hurts balmed by their belief that inclusive multiracial liberalism offered the

29

best alternative for a future South Africa. Conversely, some English-speakers decried such idealism as naivety and, in apparent contrast to the fervour with which their ancestors had supported the British Empire, now supported Afrikaner nationalism in its defence of white supremacy. The most xenophobic Afrikaners, I supposed, were away in their homes, avoiding such sinful venues as the Royal Hotel because people like me patronised them. All these factors and countless others coloured the opinions of Gatacre and the battle. Typically of South Africans, those whose views on local history were free from inherent prejudice were very few.

The prime example of such healthy objectivity, fired by a sharp mind and a ready wit, was Hennie Lotter, a slight, rather dishevelled young man with a crackling laugh. An agriculture graduate who ran several farms for his wealthy, tyrannical father, he was an intriguing contradiction: a polymath who, when drunk, praised the humanities and denigrated agriculture, yet whose knowledge of the land exceeded that of his stolid associates. Why, I often asked him, didn't he forget farming if he disliked it so much and instead seek a more amenable career? His incredulous reply never varied: he loved farming and the district was his home; he could never think of leaving. But on the few occasions when he had really considered getting out, he found that he was like someone confronted by a swaying rinkhals, mesmerised by the prospect of his inheritance.

One evening, after numerous pints, Hennie interrupted his flow of zany chatter and, completely unbidden, began to expound on Gatacre's debacle. The pivotal act, he said emphatically, was the slaughter of farmer Van Zyl's ewes by the British troops. Exhausted after a day waiting in railway trucks, exposed to the merciless summer sun at that high altitude, and after an interminable night march in full kit and with bayonets fixed, the soldiers were near to collapse as they skirted Van Zyl's homestead just before dawn. Stumbling through the lightening darkness, some stragglers did break ranks, falling asleep among the grass and kriebos. Others, ravenous and exhausted, sighted Van Zyl's ewes in their kraal and fell upon them, using their blades quickly amid the muffled bleating.

'The theft and slaughter of livestock is the cardinal sin among sheep farmers,' said Hennie. 'And Van Zyl's ewes were pregnant. That makes the khakis' actions almost sacrilege.'

Incensed, Van Zyl boldly opened fire on the culprits from his house. Pandemonium followed. Many troops, exhausted beyond rationality, suspected that they were being ambushed. In a brisk, one-sided fire-fight, the soldiers fired wildly at an imagined enemy. Meanwhile, the vanguard of Gatacre's column several hundred metres away was exchanging heavy fire with the Boers on the Kissieberg. To what extent, the question may be asked, did Gatacre's knowledge of the action behind him affect his assessment of the perilous situation in which he found himself? Later, with things going badly, was it this brief engagement near Van Zyl's homestead, and thus the idea of the chance of an outflanking movement cutting him off from Molteno, that persuaded Gatacre to pull out at that point when his Royal Irish Rifles were about to break through the Boer defences? This is a real possibility. With Gatacre's later stoical silence as to his actions that morning, we will never know for certain, but a strong case can be made for this explanation. The almost sacrilegious slaughter of the pregnant ewes by his exhausted slackers may have compounded his own violation of the Sabbath and turned fortune against him. No matter how effectively the initial setback may have been countered, the die had been cast.

Thus Hennie Lotter's explanation complemented Koos Roussouw's. Both had that depth of insight that went beyond mere manoeuvres to the very centre of the issue. For my biography to really succeed — ignoring the jibes of the more pedestrian historians — it had to assess Gatacre's destiny within, if you will, its cosmic context. Hennie's acute observation that evening in the bar fired me with enthusiasm. On we raced through a wide spectrum of subjects, each chasing its successor, like beer after beer.

Later, as I drove back to Skemerfontein with headlights

31

probing and telephone poles slipping past in the wide-domed darkness, I remember feeling exhilarated by the progress made that evening. It was the promise of just such local observations that had drawn me to the Stormberg. With more similarly oblique perceptions of Gatacre, I knew that my biography would succeed. The next morning, in penance for breaking my code of abstemiousness, I set myself an unusually long schedule and spent much of the day at work at the oak table in the sitting-room. Behind the cottage the windmill groaned, drawing sharp gushes of brackish water up from the depths as I struggled with the biography, adding brief flashes after long spells of deep concentration. Slowly, surely, like the most precise pointillist, I was adding dot after dot to my portrait of Gatacre.

Late in the afternoon, Angus Murray appeared with a gift of several mutton chops and the latest copy of the *Daily Herald*. We sat drinking tea on the verandah as he said he had done so often before with his father during the latter's reclusive retirement. Angus's reminiscences led to talk about our families and I told him the circumstances of my father's death and the floundering of my mother in Johannesburg. He, said Angus, had been particularly close to his father and greatly affected by his death. The presence of his grave in the farm cemetery, however, was reassuring to him and an affirmation of the family's commitment to Skemerfontein. More than anything else, the family graves on the farm were the reason why he could never consider selling. Even if things deteriorated as much as prophesied, he would stick it out. Atavistic and quirky though it may seem, he would not desert the graves of his forebears.

Their importance had been brought home to him the previous year when several members of the Barkhuizen family had requested permission to visit their relatives in the farm cemetery. There was, said Angus, something indescribably pitiful about the little deputation who meekly requested permission to visit the graves. Unlike graves accessible in a public cemetery, those at Skemerfontein were on Murray soil. Although the government may have made provision for such matters, ensuring access for the relatives of the interred,

Angus was determined not to place his family in the invidious position of having to request to visit its dead. Also, there was something reassuring in knowing that one's mortal remains would be interred precisely where one wanted them to be. He had never been particularly gregarious and didn't want to be hemmed in by strangers in a public plot. In her youth Olive Schreiner had chosen a lonely koppie outside Cradock for her burial place, and in spite of her death miles away near Cape Town, had been reinterred there. Like her, Angus knew that he wanted to be amongst his family, the Barkhuizens, the six Tommies and the Cape Policeman, sheltered by the cypresses and the poplars in the sloot.

The sun slipped behind Boesmanskop. Angus lit his pipe, sucking on it as the aroma of the tobacco diffused between us. Far below the lighting plant burst into life and the glow of the main homestead's lights became visible through the pines. He got up to leave and I accompanied him across the lawn to the entrance of the path that connected our two dwellings, asking him about his children as pigeons squabbled noisily for roosts on the cliff's ledges. Unhurried by the darkness, he spoke of his son and daughter, both of whom were at university: Andrew studying agriculture in Pietermaritzburg and Kate fine arts in Grahamstown. Happily, Andrew's decision to return to Skemerfontein on the completion of his degree and national service had thwarted the problem of succession.

After we parted, I returned to the cottage and lit the gas lamps. Then, a beer in hand, I made a fire in a circle of stones on the lawn and braaied the chops. The sky was clear and filled with nightjar calls. The chops sizzled on the wire grid, dripping fat onto the glowing charcoal. When they were ready, I ate them with several fistfuls of bread. The breeze sighed in the pines behind the cottage and the windmill moaned and rattled. When I had finished eating, I drank my third beer and lay back on the grass and looked up at the stars. It was blissfully peaceful.

FOUR

Sheep and Skemerfontein were as intertwined as emotions. No one, except perhaps those numbed by familiarity, could fail to notice the prevalence of the animals near the homestead or in the vast camps with their lonely troughs and windmills. No journey along the roads and tracks that meandered across the farm could avoid being confronted by swarming flocks. And no pause by an acute listener would last long before that high quietness was punctuated by a distant bleat. The sight of a large flock, advancing in hesitant sallies while being harassed by collies or kwedins, or with greater fluidity following some dull impulse of its own, was commonplace. No view was without a hint of their presence: wool tufts on barbed-wire fences; blood splatters near the diesel bowser; precise hoofprints in mud; and droppings everywhere.

From time to time flocks were driven past my cottage to a camp on the summit of the sheltering hill. Looking up from my work I would watch the milling mass advancing steadily while along its edges certain wayward members broke ranks at tangents. While these mavericks were usually overtaken and engulfed again, occasionally the flock's cohesion deteriorated sufficiently for them to break away completely. At this, a collie would bullet after them, slinking low and fast in a wide arc, cutting them off and hounding them back into the body. Bringing up the rear would be a kwedin, stick in hand, singing perhaps, or merely walking, scuffing his feet.

Often I would pan my gaze across the flock and focus on the face of a particular sheep, studying it as it moved past my window towards the pines and Bushman paintings. For the few minutes that my subject was visible I concentrated on its bland face fringed by grubby wool, noting its features and fleeting expressions: opaque eyes, pricked ears, the wrinklings along its snout, its plucking of grass and eager

34

mastication, and the opening of its mouth and the glimpse of its tongue when it bleated. And from a stance of mild contempt I began, during the course of my year on the farm, to warm towards those dull-witted creatures, observing their lambing, shearing and slaughter; in short, witnessing their blind passage down the production line that was their lives.

In fact, I learnt something new about them almost daily. From my gruesome introduction onwards, I began to realise that they weren't merely dim quadrupeds shorn annually for their fleeces but chattels upon whose total exploitation everyone on the farm depended. Like maize, sugar cane or potatoes, they were a crop to be harvested. Essentially, they were money. Consequently, their handling involved not the slightest hint of sentimentality. While orphaned lambs were bottle-fed and shut overnight in the Murrays' scullery where they could nestle in the warmth of the anthracite stove, they never came close to becoming pets. Should one be required for food, or prove consistently sickly, it summarily had its throat slit.

To my surprise, I too soon became inured to their suffering. I remember Angus and I scrutinising a grossly maimed hamel, attacked the previous night by a caracal, and discussing the behaviour of such predators for some minutes, oblivious of the extent of the sheep's suffering, before Angus ordered a labourer to put it out of its misery. Soon thereafter I also became sufficiently detached to choose one old ewe from among several, knowing that my choice meant instant death for her and that several days later I would be eating what was then alive and bleating beside me.

I have heard it said by certain vegetarians that carnivorous humans should be prepared to kill their food themselves rather than resort to the cowardly practice of delegating the task to someone else and buying meat already processed. If such an accusation needs a response, I have remained a coward. While I don't blanch at shooting game birds with a shotgun, or even despatching a wounded animal at point-blank range with a revolver, I have always disliked blades. Like the Boers — but, apparently, unlike the Tommies — I have always had a horror of cold steel.

Seeing Angus, a shotgun in hand, striding towards the shearing shed one morning not long after my arrival, I immediately assumed that another hapless sheep was about to be executed. With hindsight, I realise that my assumption was spurious because not once during my stay at Skemerfontein did I ever see him shoot more than the occasional snake and several guinea-fowl. On seeing me, he waved and crossed the yard to where I was watching several Friesland calves being fed from buckets.

'Hello Jerry. I'm just going to sort out a puff adder. Why don't you come along,' he said, his face bisected by the shadow of his slouch hat.

'Thanks,' I replied, accompanying him, striding past the dipping tank and towards the silos.

The labourers, he said, had been complaining for weeks about a large puff adder in the old silo. They had tried to kill it but on each occasion the snake had escaped into the rat warren beneath the sacks. Ten minutes previously, before going to get mealies for the stud rams, one of the labourers had seen it curled up on the sacks and had called him. It was a pity, said Angus, that the snake had to be killed at all because it had to be living off rats, but the danger it posed made it necessary.

On reaching the silo, Angus spoke in Xhosa to one of the several waiting labourers who pointed through the partly open door. Crouching beside him, Angus peered down onto the mounds of sacks in the gloom. He nodded and beckoned me, and I too peered down and saw the dark coil against the lighter grey shadow of the hessian. Then, crouching on the threshold of the small doorway, he gestured us away and aimed down into the darkness. Waiting with the labourers behind him I braced myself for the blast. When it came, it was louder than expected, magnified by the hollow interior of the nearly empty silo.

When the haze of dust and chaff had cleared partly, he pushed wide open the small door with the tip of the barrels and descended the metal-runged ladder to the silo floor, returning presently with the adder. The fine pellets had almost obliterated the snake's head, onto which several mealie grains had become encrusted.

'Look how fat it is,' he said, extending an arm from which the snake hung limply like eighteen inches of putrifying salami. 'I'll get one of the chaps to cut it open so we can see what it's been eating.' He flopped the snake onto the ground and spoke to his headman in Xhosa.

Taking a pen-knife from his pocket (the same tartan-handled knife, I noticed, that he had used to slit the ewe's throat several weeks previously), the headman inserted its tip into the snake's cloaca, ripped a long gash down the middle of its underside, and removed from its stomach what looked like two bedraggled mice. Braving the stench, I squatted and craned forward with Angus who prodded the creatures with a twig. Finding what looked like wings, he prised them open.

'Crikey,' he exclaimed, 'they're little starlings. The blighter must have got them after they'd fallen out of a nest in the eaves.'

Lapsing momentarily into anthropomorphism, I imagined the terror of the fledglings as they watched the blunt triangular head weaving towards them, its yellow eyes impassive and its tongue flickering in anticipation.

'Thanks,' he said to the headman. 'You can throw it away now.' The man skewered the snake on a stick and, walking some distance towards the grove of poplars behind the stud rams' enclosure, flicked it into the undergrowth between the silver trunks.

'Let's go and have a cup of tea,' said Angus, and we retraced our steps across the yard towards the large stone farmhouse with the sunlight bouncing brightly off its green, corrugated-iron roof.

Entering via the kitchen, Angus requested tea, and soon an aproned maid appeared and placed the tray on a table in the study. Mary then joined us and we sat back in arm chairs and nattered, encircled by high bookshelves and assorted bric-a-brac: Anglo-Boer War shell cases, a stuffed korhaan, and rosettes and cups won at various agricultural shows. As we talked a bee began buzzing and butting against a sash window until Angus stopped cleaning his shotgun and released it. Then, our voices punctuated only by crockery sounds, we continued, the Murrays and I displaying an ease and familiarity with each other that belied the fact that I had been at Skemerfontein for little over a month.

Presently Mary announced that she had to return to her letter writing. Standing up as she left, I noticed a family photograph partly hidden among copies of the *Farmer's Weekly* on Angus's desk. Obviously taken not long previously, it pictured the four Murrays in swimming costumes on a beach with a large casuarina behind them.

'So this is the complete family,' I said jocularly, pointing at the portrait.

'Oh yes,' he said almost diffidently, the stock of the shotgun in his hand. 'It was taken when we were on holiday in Natal last year.'

'Your children look very nice,' I continued, immediately embarrassed by the banality of my observation.

'Yes,' he laughed, 'they are.'

Andrew was a pleasant looking youth with his mother's fair hair and a broad face devoid of hints of complexity; a face, in short, well suited to an agricultural student. Katie, however, gave a very different impression. While her strong, fine features and plaited auburn hair were unashamedly European, the sunburnt nose and necklace of Zulu beads, caught beneath the casuarina branches, revealed glimpses of something distinctly African. The mere sight of her in the photograph was epiphanic. From that moment onwards, I desired her.

What it is about Katie that I find so alluring is hard to define. Watching her painting on the front verandah as I write this, I can offer only a suggestion. Far more than just her striking face and slim voluptuousness, her beauty is a compendium of those ageless clichés and contradictions beloved of the smitten: self-containment and vulnerability, hautiness and humility, delicacy of manner and inklings of wantonness. Also embroiled are affections which we have in common: for her parents, Skemerfontein and, most importantly, for that whole world in which Gatacre, when so nearly victorious, stumbled and fell.

38

FIVE

During the next three and a half decades, barring interludes in Burma and England, Gatacre was stationed in India. Using Beatrix's eulogy (among other less impassioned sources), I followed his progress from subaltern to brigadier on that subcontinent, always wary of his devoted widow's subjectivity, like a diligent journalist reworking an advertising handout excising most superlatives in search of the truth. For this account, not wanting a cumbersome chronology but local colour and a glimpse of the Gatacre persona, I have been recklessly selective, using a pastiche in the hope that from it will emerge a true likeness.

Dominant during those years, as always, was that obsession with athleticism which was later to contribute to his undoing in the Stormberg. Seeking more than the already vigorous life of a professional soldier, he jumped at opportunities of adventure: riding, hiking and visiting temples, sketching, painting in watercolours, and shooting obsessively: black and brown bears, deer, ibex, barrasingh buck, snipe; almost anything, it appears, that moved. Often startling was the juxtaposition of the disparate elements – the *Boys' Own* bravado and the awestruck aestheticism – revealing a dichotomy in his nature, as the following extracts from his letters show.

Reval, May 16, 1867
Fine morning at last; put everything in the sun to dry. Went out shooting after breakfast, and had a good day; killed a black bear about 200 yards from camp. Had a shot at an ibex; saw nine, but did not hit one. Slept under a tree for about an hour; on my way back killed a brown bear with a beautiful silvery skin, and hit a barrasingh buck in the chest; tracked him a long way, found some blood. Night was coming on and it began

to rain, so had to give up the search or should probably have got him . . . In jumping across the stream I fell in and got wet through; water very strong, was carried down like an arrow; caught hold of a stone and came ashore, took off my things and stood in the sun to dry: sketch reserved.

Rupshu Salt Lakes, (c. 1867)
The distance I came today was fifty-eight miles; I was nearly dead with fever, and sun and cold, and walking, and riding in a wooden saddle all day.

Baltal, July 1, 1867
There are waterfalls from nearly every rock, which looks very pretty and the water is such as 'only tee-totallers desire or deserve'. The wild roses, white, red, and yellow, are covered with blossoms, and their smell is delicious.

Camp Hamurghuri, December 18, 1881
We are having a very pleasant march from Nusserabad to Neemuch; good shooting all the way — duck, snipe, and deer; also some capital pig-sticking. The wild boars here are very difficult to get out of the jungle and grass, but when one does get them out across the open ground they run like greyhounds. . . . When you get up to them they turn round and run back a pace or two, and then come straight at you, rising on their hind legs to cut your horse if they get the chance, but this of course they can't do if you use your spear properly. I have got some capital tushes. The best run we had as yet was at a place called Roopauli, two marches back; two boars broke cover together and went away over capital ground to another place two miles off. The Commander in Chief [General the Honourable Arthur Hardinge, CiC of the Bombay Army] and I took one and had a capital run after him. I had the luck to get the first spear. I was pleased, because I was riding a horse of the Chief's that could never be got up to a pig before.

This is a beautiful country to march through, very long grass and jungle all round; nearly all the hills are of white marble and spotted marble of sorts, and an enormous number of old forts and temples beautifully ornamented with carvings in marble and stone. Some of them are extraordinarily beautiful in form and design of carving, far superior to anything we see now — and these are thousands, not hundreds, of years old.

Bannu, (c. 1887)
There was much game along the route [of a proposed new road from Loralai to Dera Ghazi Khan on the Indus]: markhor, a large goat with splendid horns; gud, a large sheep with very large curly horns, wolves and small game, hares, partridges, wood-pigeons, etc. I had very little time for shooting, but shot one markhor and much small game here and there as I came across it; but as I had a lot of surveying to do all day, I had no time to make excursions after game alone . . . You would have been delighted with the country in some places, something like Scotland with fewer trees and more sun, but comparatively cool for India. The only disagreeable thing about it is the general want of water and the number of poisonous snakes . . . The snakes are everywhere, and it was a few days before I left Khur that a young engineer named Hackman was bitten. I saw his death in yesterday's paper. I killed several cobras while marching, I am glad to say.

Have the opposing traits begun to emerge? If not, immerse yourself again in the preceding extracts and ferret out the polarisation. As it emerges, separate the athleticism from the aestheticism, placing all mention of shooting, walking, riding and pig-sticking in one category and pretty waterfalls, the delicious smell of wild roses and the exquisite ornamentation of marble temples in another. Then ask yourself these questions: How powerful was Gatacre's aestheticism? To what extent did it need suppression by his soldierly side? Was its containment the root of his restlessness? And, had his athlet-

41

icism been unchallenged, would his agitation have been tempered? Of course no real conclusion can be drawn from so brief a glimpse, but I am convinced that these questions hold the key.

In the extracts that follow are scattered further clues to the dichotomy, among other characteristics: his bravery (or foolhardiness?), his enthusiasm for horticulture, his delight in his athletic prowess, and his abiding passion for soldiering which he attempted to convince Beatrix was less than his passion for her.

Simla, September, 1887
Did I tell you I was nearly polished off by a madman with a revolver? He shot two men he came across, then got onto a rock and defied the crowd, but I got a stick and went for him, to prevent his doing more mischief. He warned me not to come near him, but I spoke to him in his own language, and never took my eyes off him, and when he was going to have a shot at me he suddenly changed his mind and blew a hole in his breast about three inches in diameter. The fact was he was not quite sure whether he had a spare round for himself, and these fanatical fellows always destroy themselves after doing as much mischief as they are able; when he shot himself I was just within reach of him, but too late to knock the pistol out of his hands.

In the defile just below Bhamo, Burma, February 8, 1890
There is a great charm to me in going into quite an unknown country [on an expedition into the Kachin Hills to crush a band of dacoits], full of wild beasts and savages; there is nearly every animal under the sun said to be in these jungles, and the place has every appearance of it: tracks of all sorts along the river-banks. But we shall soon see for ourselves. I fancy the scenery will be grand and we shall probably get many beautiful orchids.

The Palace, Mandalay, July 22, 1890
I have got influenza, which is a great nuisance, as it keeps me from my work, and the doctor warns me solemnly not to go in draughts and to keep out of the sun; but as my present abode is merely a large gilt shed, about thirty yards square, with looking-glass panels open to the four winds of heaven, it is rather difficult to follow his advice . . .

I wish I had the services of Payn for a bit in the palace gardens: I would make them so pretty. We have rocks, grass, water, everything that one could wish to work upon, but have no artistic people who understand gardening. I am working at it, and getting seeds, and I hope to make it a pretty place by-and-by.

Bombay, December, 1894
I am always thinking of how I can get on, not for the sake of the money it brings, but for soldiering itself.

Bombay, December, 1894
I hope you [Beatrix] will not mind my love for soldiering and work; it has such a fascination for me, I am inclined to put it first always. But my love for you will stand out first, and your love for me will enable me to carry out my work at personal inconvenience to ourselves, won't it? You see I am cunningly trying to get you to overlook my endeavours to think of soldiering as the first thing, but, dear, you will always be in my heart all the time.

Bombay, December 21, 1894
I have fever this morning; have not had any sleep for days, and had to run in the Open Competition for Officers' Tent-pegging, which I won easily, taking both pegs and then touching two more turned on edge. I was rather pleased, as no one else touched one sideways at all, and all were about twenty years younger than I!

Lowari Pass, (c. 1895)
Yesterday after passing over the pass we found on the
hills along which the road ran all English flowers — nar-
cissus, iris, lilies (they plant them on their graves), may,
hawthorn, hyacinths, tulips, in great profusion. The
country is magnificent, soil very rich, would grow
anything; we must take the country and improve it.

Lowari Pass, (c. 1895)
I had a hard day the day before yesterday. My orderly
officer and I had to go from Dir to Janbatai and back,
about fifty-six miles over a difficult road; we started
at 5a.m. and did not get back till 1a.m. yesterday. For
we were delayed on the road so long inspecting that
night overtook us, and we had to walk along a most impossible track leading our ponies; we literally had to
feel our way with our feet. We all got falls over rocks
and stones, but beyond breaking our skin and clothes
we were none the worse. The river was running under us
nearly all the way about 300 ft straight down, so you
may imagine we had to be careful.

What sort of composite emerges? That of a spartan martinet
with a softer side exposed only in these personal letters?
Perhaps, but we mustn't forget devoted Beatrix's partiality
as it was she who chose the selection from which the above
quotes were taken. And it must be remembered that all was
not idolatry. Gatacre always had his critics, and towards
the end of his Indian years his nature revealed a trait of
foolhardiness that gave them ample ammunition. Admirable
though reckless bravery may be in a soldier of lesser rank,
there is something disturbing about a brigadier and district
commander curtailing his leave and *with only five sepoys and
a local guide* risking his life to arrest a band of murderers
in the hills outside Quetta.

As it happened, Gatacre survived the fracas and no attempt
was made on his life by the desperate and inadequately
guarded prisoners on the return journey to Quetta, but his
actions earned him a barbed compliment from General Sir

George White, then Commander in Chief of India and later the commanding officer of the British force besieged in Ladysmith. Congratulating Gatacre, White said how glad he was to know that he had under him generals who 'take to the hills for amusement' but added that had Gatacre been killed, the whole affair would have taken on a 'sinister importance'. However, concluded the CiC on a half-conciliatory note, 'all is well that ends well'.

Apart from his military and administrative duties — among other things, he was a member of the Hazara Field Force, a brigade commander in the Chitral Expedition and Bombay's commanding officer during its plague of 1896–97 — there are many more labels that could be attached to Gatacre during those decades: among them, secretary to a mutton and poultry club; keeper of a quailery; father of three sons, one of whom died in infancy; inventor of a mess tin; visitor to the world's second largest bell; jockey in regimental races; supplicant to the Burra Lama; discoverer of a fern which was later named after him; actor in amateur farces; deserted husband (by his first wife, Alice); and imagined victim of rabies.

Understandably, someone as devoted as Beatrix makes only brief reference to the painful dissolution of her husband's first marriage and his encounter with a supposedly rabid jackal. However, that both occurred at much the same time is significant as their combined impact seemed temporarily to unhinge Gatacre, who complained of nightmares teeming with howling jackals and locked his bedroom door and had bars placed across the windows as a precaution. Needless to say, neither the jackals attacked, nor did he die of rabies, and it was the timely arrival of his beloved Beatrix that brought him back from the brink.

These hiccups apart, it must be noted that Gatacre left India for Britain at a high point in his life. Largely through his administrative skill, the spread of the Bombay plague had been arrested and the epidemic contained, and many Indians and Europeans saw in him a saviour and a man destined for greatness. That his career, built so painstakingly over those Indian decades, would in three years be shattered, was a thought too wildly irrational even to be dreamed of.

SIX

On recollection, I can detect a close connection between my occasional bouts of gloom and my visits to the Royal Hotel. At the first intimations of darkness I found myself being propelled through those batwing doors into the smoky conviviality where, primed with alcohol, I established an acquaintanceship with a broad selection of the regulars. Our topics of conversation were usually limited to small-town trivia, stereotypical political views and bawdiness, a repertoire which soon palled although there remained something remarkable about the delusions from which most of their exponents suffered. Perhaps it was the alcohol that gave them the courage to dismiss the impending cataclysm in this country which so preoccupies the world at large. Or perhaps they were merely those people who blunder blindly through life, oblivious of the future; the kind that makes up the throngs of refugees escaping bloodshed when those of their counterparts who had been wracked by anxiety over the preceding years had long seen the writing on the wall and had taken the gap. Whatever the reasons for their bluff nonchalance, I found their company uplifting on those occasions when I was down. I enjoyed the scandal, the political clichés and the rude jokes. They relieved me of the demands of my task, relegating Gatacre to the sidelines while we made merry.

One evening nearing midnight, after the bar had closed and those of us who had been evicted stood shouting incoherently at each other on the pavement outside, Hennie Lotter demanded that I accompany him to visit a friend of his. Brandishing a bottle of brandy like a cosh, he set off unsteadily along the main street, passing a dozing night watchman outside the Co-op, while I followed as hotly as my own unsteadiness permitted. Turning left up a side street towards the station, Hennie took a gravel path towards a row of redbrick cottages alongside the railway tracks, slowly mounting the steps outside the furtherest. Handing the bottle to me, he began rapping sharply on the door and a window beside it, calling 'Martie, Martie', Martie' and hiccuping intermittently. Then he paused briefly, resting his forehead against the wall, before gesticulating for the bottle, taking a slug, and muttering in Afrikaans: 'Jussus! She sleeps like a dead sheep.'

Fortified, he attacked the door again, only to be stilled by an irritated voice from within: 'Wait man Hennie, I'm just putting my clothes on.'

'Fuck your clothes,' he shouted, turning towards me and convulsing with a combined guffaw and hiccups.

A few minutes later the door opened and a young, blonde woman in a pink towelling dressing gown appeared. On seeing me, she started momentarily, but Hennie kissed her and explained in Afrikaans: 'This,' he said, gesturing and then clasping my shirt, 'is my good friend Jerry. He's come all the way from Durban for a good time.'

'Hello,' she said, stepping back and opening the door. Hennie entered and I followed. On the way to the sitting-room he caressed her buttocks, smoothing them with an open hand. Inside it was dark except for a glass ornament on a hi-fi cabinet from whose translucent centre radiated a succession of coloured lights. Settling in a vinyl armchair I watched Hennie and Martie on a sofa opposite me, focusing on her décolletage, engrossed in its transformation from red to green to yellow to blue, then red again, and so on, endlessly, as the coloured lights lapped in wavelets across the room. Somewhat sobered by our brisk walk from the hotel, I crossed to the hi-fi and put on a Dire Straits record. Hennie offered me a drink from the sofa and, when I declined, took a slug himself, filling a tumbler with equal proportions of brandy and Coke for Martie who gulped it down, grimacing like a child taking medicine. They then began to fondle each other and I dozed off, deep in my chair, submerged by the music.

For how long I had been asleep I don't know, but I was woken by Martie unbuttoning my shirt and pecking a ladder of kisses from my neck to my navel. Her mussed hair was in my face and through it I could see Hennie lying on the sofa, his gentle snoring audible whenever the music softened.

47

When she lifted her head to kiss me on the mouth I noticed that her dressing gown was open and that her full breasts were hanging like prize aubergines in the glow of blue light from the glass ornament.

'Hennie,' she whispered in hesitant English, momentarily disengaging her lips, 'said I must be nice to you.'

That assurance was all I needed. Jerking upright in the chair I returned her embrace, toppling both of us like acrobats in tandem onto the furry carpet. There we kissed and fondled, contorting quickly out of our remaining clothing. Fired by our nakedness, we caressed more intimately, quickening the tempo. Then, suddenly, she halted, pushing me back onto my knees. Bewildered, I paused, poised, fearful that she'd had a change of heart. Instead, she did something that has always struck me as strange: slowly, deliberately, breaking the momentum, she settled herself on her back on the carpet, raised her bent legs towards the ceiling and parted them as wide as seemed possible before beckoning me onto her.

The effect was extraordinary. Apart from the abrupt drop in tempo, her movements suggested a metamorphosis: the long, sinuous form beside me on the carpet had buckled and fanned out limbs. As we began to couple, splashed by the waves of colour, her transformation called to mind a distant but apposite image.

It was late at night in the guard tent in the bush during my national service. On a metal table was a gas lamp and an urn of coffee, long since cooled. Returning from my beat with a fellow guard, we filled our tin mugs with coffee and balanced them on the gas lamp to be heated. As we sat waiting at the table, our rifles beside us, chewing army biscuits, the lamp hissing and hyenas whooping and giggling in the distance, we were mesmerised by the antics of scores of little beetles. Attracted by the light, many circled the lamp itself, the most adventurous moving too close and being shrivelled by the heat, while others scurried zigzaggedly across the table-top. Periodically, we noticed, each insect stopped and fluttered its wings briefly, then exploded, flicking itself upwards in a tight somersault and landing contorted on its back. Seemingly stunned, each maintained this awkward posture for several seconds, then rolled over, unravelled itself and resumed its bustling.

Years later on the floor of that railway cottage in the Eastern Cape, my brain tenuously linked those beetle somersaults with Martie's mutation and the image lingered as we coupled; and afterwards, on my withdrawal, Martie too rolled over and unravelled herself before disappearing down the passage. Vaguely, I recollect the sound of a lavatory flushing, and then I fell asleep.

The next thing I remember was Martie shaking me awake, imploring me to leave immediately as her train-driver father would be back soon. As I pulled on my clothes, I noticed that Hennie was no longer on the sofa, and that with the beginnings of dawn creeping around the curtains, the room looked singularly drab and sad.

I next met Martie in the pharmacy several weeks later. Having gone in to buy some minor necessity, I was surprised to find her helping behind the counter. Trim and attractive in her white uniform, she greeted me cheerily, showing none of the embarrassment that I would have expected after our encounter. In fact her manner was almost coquettish: she regarded me boldly and, bending down beside me to retrieve something from the floor, appeared briefly to present herself in the manner of female animals on heat. I doubt whether both these observations went beyond mere wishfulness, but there was definitely an air of intimacy between us that could easily have been suppressed.

'Come and see me sometime,' she said on parting, which I did the following week after another binge at the hotel. Taking the side street and skirting the station platform, I stumbled along the gravel path and up the steps to the front door. After knocking repeatedly, with no answer, I peered in the nearest window. There were no curtains and in the moonlight I saw that the room was empty. Nothing remained of the scene of our encounter except several sheets of newspaper on the scarred floorboards. The effect was uncanny: as if that portion of the past had been excised, had never happened, and that all memories of it were illusory.

Hennie informed me later that Martie's father had absconded to avoid zealous creditors and that Martie had accompanied him. Rumour had it that they had gone to Johannesburg. While Hennie was flippant about Martie's departure, I was disappointed. I had assumed, naively perhaps, that a relationship of sorts could have been established. But I never saw her again. It was celibacy until Katie came.

SEVEN

Most of the preceding chapter came to me slowly in my study one sweltering afternoon last week. I wrote each sentence in longhand as an electric fan strove vainly to disperse the mugginess, moving from side to side like the shaking head of an incredulous bystander. During my frequent pauses, I was particularly aware of the thunder of the breakers and the skirl of cicadas; only they seemed to have any animation. Even Katie had succumbed and was asleep in the hammock between the palms. Determined to press on, I added sentence to sentence, grappling with the past until quite unexpectedly the tempo began to change. What heralded this was my recollection of the manner of Martie's spread-eagling and the resultant connection made with those acrobatic beetles in the guard tent during my national service.

On the completion of that lateral move and my return to the narrative, one feature of that earlier period remained: my fellow guard that evening, one Garry Stander, who inexplicably chose me as a confidant as we wove through the mopanis in the darkness. Whispering domestic confidences, he told me of the tragedy of his mother, oblivious that several days later he was to add to it his own. Committed last week to Martie's story, I pushed this diversion aside, but it has persisted and is worth including. From what I can remember, including a little improvisation, it went like this.

One evening Garry's mother came back from the laundromat earlier than expected to find that the bedroom door was locked. She listened and heard her husband inside with another woman. She shouted at them to come out, saying that she knew what they were doing. His father shouted back that they would come out when they were finished. The woman inside giggled. Garry's mother started sobbing. She crossed to the drinks cabinet and gulped down a half-jack of vodka. Then she collapsed sobbing on the couch. When

51

she wiped the tears with the back of her hand, she smudged mascara above her eyes.

After about half an hour her husband and the other woman came out of the bedroom. He was in shorts and a vest and the young woman fell back a little so that she was half behind him when Garry's mother looked up at them from the sofa. The other woman had a silly grin on her face. She was wearing a T-shirt with 'Pussycat' written across it in big red letters. Garry's mother started screaming at them in her slurred voice and his father shouted at her to shut up. She just carried on screaming. His father shouted that he was going to walk his lady friend home and if she didn't shut up he'd give her a thrashing when he got back. He pulled the glass sliding door to one side and let the blonde woman go through first. Garry's mother started screaming even louder and ran up behind them and tried to kick the other woman as she stepped out onto the patio. Because she was drunk and wearing high-heels, she missed and put her foot through the glass door. She fell to the ground screaming. Blood started pouring out of her leg. Garry's father shouted out over his shoulder that it served her right and disappeared to walk the other woman home. While Garry and his younger brother tried to staunch the bleeding with their dressing-gowns, his mother bled to death. There was even blood on the patio although she was still in the lounge.

Garry said that he hated his father so much that he didn't care if he was dead. He had heard that he was working on a mine in Zimbabwe. Garry and his brother had been brought up by his mother's mother and father who lived in Benoni. He said that he felt like a cigarette and we sneaked one each in the trees below the camp. The river was just below us and we could hear hippos grunting and crashing about in the reeds. While we were smoking, he put down his rifle to show me the place just above the ankle where his mother had been cut. All he wanted to do now, he said, was to find a steady wife and become a mechanic and live peacefully near his mother's parents. He had it all planned in his head. He said he would set up speakers in his garage so that he could listen to music while he was working on cars in the evenings.

And then his wife would bring him a cold beer from the fridge and she would sit and talk to him while he was working. We only had fourteen months left in the army and then, he said, he would start setting himself up. I said that it sounded like a great idea.

'Let's drink to it,' he said, pulling a bottle of cane out of his webbing. I asked him where he had got it from and he said that he had smuggled it in in his duffel bag and had just been waiting for a good time to drink it.

'Hell no,' I said to him, 'Garry, much as I would like to share it with you, they'll throw us in DB if we get pissed on guard duty.' I reminded him that for every day we spent in DB, we would have to do an additional day of national service which would delay his plans to get himself organised. He put the bottle away but promised that he would share it with me because we'd had such a good chat. We shook on it.

The next time we were on guard duty together was three days later and although we tried to be on the same beat, he got the first beat at the armoury while I got the second. The armoury guard stands alone and Garry seemed quite upset, saying that he felt like another good chat. I told him not to worry about it because we could arrange to be on the same beat when it was next our turn the following week.

I stood from eight to ten at the armoury and then went to sleep in the guard tent with my rifle and pistol beside me on the camp-bed. The authorities kept on about your rifle being your wife and I could feel her beside me with the coldness of her flash-hider up against my cheek.

The guard commander woke the second beat at about ten to two and I set off through the tents to the rondavel which was serving as the armoury. I expected to find Garry but there was no sign of him. I called out softly so that the guard commander wouldn't hear me. When there was no reply, I began my beat, assuming that he must have left early for the guard tent. Although the guard being relieved had to hand over to his successor, he probably hadn't bothered because he knew it was going to be me. I began to walk slowly round and round the rondavel. The hippos were crashing about down near the river and I remember noting how similar their grunts were to those made by pigs.

I hadn't been pushing long when someone holding a pistol jumped out of the shadows and shouted at me to stick my hands up. I froze and flicked the safety catch of my rifle off before I realised that it was Garry. From the way he had shouted I knew that he had drunk his bottle of cane. I told him to keep the noise down and to put the pistol away because he would be in big trouble if the guard commander caught him. And I reminded him about DB and how he would have to do the days over again and how that would delay his setting himself up. He laughed and waved the pistol around.

'Garry,' I shouted at him as quietly as I could, 'put that bloody pistol away.'

'This,' he shouted, looking at the pistol in his hand, 'is a useless piece of junk. I couldn't shoot my balls off with it if I tried.' He pointed it at his crotch and began to laugh so that his shoulders heaved.

'Jesus, Garry.' I lunged and made a grab for it as he pulled the trigger. The bullet ripped open his scrotum and blew his balls to pieces. We bandaged him up and a medic drove him in a Land Rover to the doctor at the base camp some twenty miles away. They sewed him up that night and I visited him at the military hospital several days later. He was lying in bed and was very pale and in pain. I asked him how he was and he said that he had been charged with drunkenness on guard duty and damage to state property. I said I was very sorry and that I would visit him again soon.

I never saw Garry Stander again and I often wonder if he became a mechanic and if he set himself up in a house near his grandparents and if he and his wife adopted children and she brought him cold beers from the fridge when he was working on his car in the garage in the evenings. From time to time I have met people with the same surname and have asked them if they have a relative called Garry, but never with any luck. If this account of my stay at Skemerfontein and my quest for Gatacre is ever published, perhaps Garry may read it and be reminded of that evening in the guard tent when we watched those little beetles and the marvellous way in which they somersaulted.

EIGHT

No sooner had Gatacre returned home from India and begun to enjoy English life again than he was called up for active service in the Sudan. For thirteen years Britain had bridled at the killing in Khartoum of General Gordon and the ignominious retreat of its troops from the territory, but had done nothing. Now, fearful of intervention by other powers and glad of an opportunity to settle an old score, a new Conservative government had sanctioned a punitive expedition under General Kitchener, Sirdar of the Egyptian Army.

Advancing up the Nile, Kitchener was determined to engage the Khalifa's army and completely destroy the Dervish Empire. To achieve this he had his army of Egyptian and Sudanese troops led by British officers, and the support of a single British brigade which Gatacre had been chosen to command.

Of Gatacre's entrance into the North African arena, Winston Churchill, an enduring admirer, said the following:

> The officer selected for the command of the British brigade was a man of high character and ability. General Gatacre had already led a brigade in the Chitral expedition. He left India, leaving behind him golden opinions, just before the outbreak of the great Frontier rising, and was appointed to a brigade at Aldershot. Thence we now find him hurried to the Sudan — a spare, middle-sized man, of great physical strength and energy, of marked capacity and unquestioned courage, but disturbed by a restless irritation, which often left him the exhausted victim of his own vitality.

Setting out early on January 5, 1898, Gatacre travelled from Charing Cross Station, via Marseilles, to Egypt where he joined his brigade as it marched southwards along a railway line which was simultaneously being built. Consequently, the brigade's advance was like that of a caterpillar, bunching up and extending in alternate movements. Whenever delays forced a halt, as at Abu Dis, Gatacre drilled his troops mercilessly, honing their fitness and efficiency but inviting criticism for his alleged excesses. Other hindrances were bullets which required modification to increase their stopping power and the need to replace boots which had been shredded by the harsh terrain.

Once again Gatacre's letters, as chosen by Beatrix, are invaluable, providing incisive personal flashes among the reams of military data. As in India, these epistles reveal much of the non-military man, especially his naturalism, the Indian tree rooted in the Claverley countryside having grafted to the harsh desert landscape. As it would be cumbersome in this brief memoir to include every letter used in the biography, a short medley will have to suffice, stringing together a naturalist martinet's interior monologue as he leads his troops towards Omdurman and retribution:

Such a desert — not a thing to be seen but sand and a few black rocks jutting out of the plain. A few straw-coloured birds, like stonechats, and a wagtail I saw at one place; goodness knows what they live on ... There are crocodiles in the river here, but not many. A fisherman caught one about three feet long, a most vicious little brute, who snaps at everyone and everything; he is tied by the middle with a piece of string, and swims about in a bath; he will probably be eaten when his master gets hungry ... Three days ago a gazelle was trapped and sent in to us by a native. He was uninjured, and a beautiful little brute, with large eyes. We all decided to keep him as a pet, and he got quite tame in a few hours. But alas! we got hungry, and someone suggested that he might escape — so we ate him. Perhaps it was the wisest course.

Like Angus's naturalism, you will note, Gatacre's was that of a countryman: without sentimentality, with aesthetics and necessity rubbing shoulders.

Wanting to test the strength of the infidel, the Khalifa ordered one of his emirs, a certain Mahmud, to confront the advancing column with a force of twenty thousand Dervishes. Receiving instructions to advance, Gatacre did so with characteristic zest, in three days marching his troops some seventy miles across yielding sand and rocky outcrops to within striking distance of the Dervish camp at Atbara. Next followed an exasperating delay, during which an impatient Gatacre badgered an indecisive Kitchener until the go-ahead was given. Leaving their bivouac on the evening preceding the battle, the twelve thousand British and Egyptian troops marched through the night to Atbara, arriving at dawn on a plateau above the Dervishes' camp with its encircling zeriba. There, after an artillery bombardment, they attacked, the Lincoln Regiment and Cameron and Seaforth Highlanders shouting 'Remember Gordon' as they swept down the slope to the sound of pipes, fifes and drums. Deployed in a long line and firing continuously, the troops met a scythe of lead as they neared the zeriba, yet managed to dismantle a section of the thorns and breach the defences. What followed was almost surreal: refusing to run, the defeated Dervishes, their robes fluttering, strode away across the desert and were potted like winged partridges.

For the British, Atbara was a decisive victory, but not without cost. While the Dervishes were routed, with over three thousand killed, and the hapless Mahmud captured, the Anglo-Egyptian Army suffered about six hundred casualties, among them some very good officers and men. About this Gatacre was philosophical, regretting their loss but conceding that such was war. He cut locks of hair from two dead captains of the Camerons but was unable to get sufficient hair from the closely cropped head of another officer. Then all the dead were buried in one grave. The pipers and buglers of a Sudanese battalion played the Dead March from 'Saul', followed by the pipers of the Camerons and Seaforths with a lament before sand was shovelled onto the corpses.

During the attack, Gatacre was conspicuous for his almost demonic fervour. At the head of his battalion, he ignored the withering fire and was among the first to reach the zeriba and begin dismantling it. As with his pursuit and arrest of the band of murderers in the hills outside Quetta two years previously, such rashness by a commanding officer provoked censure. Among those to notice this flaw was Arthur Conan Doyle, who wrote the following perceptive description:

General Gatacre [was] a man who bore a high reputation for fearlessness and tireless energy, though he had been criticised, notably during the Sudan campaign, for having called upon his men for undue and unnecessary exertion. 'General Back-acher' they called him, with rough soldierly chaff. A glance at his long thin figure, his gaunt Don Quixote face, and his aggressive jaw would show his personal energy, but might not satisfy the observer that he possessed those intellectual gifts which qualify for high command. At the action at Atbara he, the brigadier in command, was the first to reach and tear down the zereeba [sic] of the enemy — a gallant exploit of the soldier, but a questionable position for the general. The man's strength and his weakness lay in the incident.

Kitchener, however, was delighted with Gatacre, lauding him for his untiring energy and gallant leadership.

With the benefit of hindsight accorded the biographer, I have found two more features of the battle of Atbara which bear mentioning. The first was the night march from Abadar to the Dervish encampment, the efficacy of which must have influenced Gatacre's fateful decision to repeat the tactic under different circumstances in the Stormberg the following year. The other is the date of the battle: April 8, 1898, a Good Friday. With the Dervishes being Muslims, Gatacre couldn't have hoped for the unpreparedness of devotees, but here may be the origin of his apparent preference for action on religious holidays, both Omdurman and Stormberg having been fought on Sundays.

For the Anglo-Egyptian army there followed a three-month delay before the final thrust to Omdurman. Waiting in the searing heat for the level of the Nile to rise sufficiently to carry steamers upstream, the troops made preparations and killed time with scorpion and spider fights. Gatacre took a fortnight's leave in Cairo and Alexandria, during which he received notification that his rank of major general had been made substantive, and that he had been promoted from brigade to divisional command. A further brigade of British troops arrived with two colonels: Lyttelton to lead the reinforcements and Wauchope to replace Gatacre. Both men, as generals in the Anglo-Boer War, met very different fates: Lyttelton was among the few successful British commanders, and was promoted during the war, while Wauchope was killed leading the Highland Brigade at Magersfontein the day after Gatacre's Stormberg debacle.

As a consequence of his promotion, Gatacre saw little action for the remainder of the Sudan campaign. Now one of Kitchener's headquarters staff, he was compelled to watch the fray from a distance rather than bloody his hands. For this reason we must, like a movie camera, withdraw into the sky for a bird's-eye view of the remaining hostilities.

Eventually the advance began, the troops travelling by steamer and barge to within fifty-five miles of Omdurman, and then continuing on foot. Stopping at a village called Egeiga, a short distance north of the city, and fearing a night attack by the Khalifa, Kitchener had his troops prepare defensive positions and local villagers spread the word that he was taking the offensive after dark. This ploy worked, keeping the Dervishes at bay until dawn when some ten thousand of them, led by the ferocious Osman Azrak, attacked. After waiting for them to enter range, the British let loose with field guns, rifles and maxims, felling the screaming horde for three quarters of an hour until the attack finally faltered. Next came a renewed assault from the right, which was similarly repulsed. Once again, the retreating Dervishes refused to run and were potted like game by the victors.

Knowing, however, that half of the Khalifa's force had yet to be engaged, and wanting to reach Omdurman before nightfall, Kitchener resumed the advance in the hope of provoking a confrontation. Sent forward as a precautionary measure, the 21st Lancers reconnoitred the route and detected what appeared to be a small group of Dervishes whom they promptly charged. Discovering too late that the force was in fact two thousand strong, the cavalry continued, galloping through them with lances lunging, and then re-formed and charged back again.

While this minor diversion was of no real military significance, its glorious foolhardiness achieved a mythic status and earned VCs for three of its participants, one of whom was the dashing Lieutenant Jim de Montmorency whose fate in the Stormberg, as we shall see, was inextricably linked to Gatacre's.

The remaining half of the Dervish army then attacked Kitchener's force from all sides. Discarding the command chain, the Sirdar himself assumed complete control and after a period of sustained rifle fire from the defenders, the Dervishes retreated in disarray.

After an hour and a half's rest, the Anglo-Egyptians headed for Omdurman which they entered during the afternoon, offering clemency to women, children and the aged if all arms were surrendered. The city's resistance was minimal and after dark Kitchener left its fetid confines and bivouacked in the desert outside.

In all, the day's fighting had cost Kitchener's army a mere forty-eight dead, of whom twenty-three were British. Eleven thousand Dervish dead were strewn across the desert, with sixteen thousand taken prisoner. Such a staggering disparity in losses could only have bolstered further the British conviction of their superiority, ill preparing them for what lay ahead the following year at the foot of the continent.

Throughout the day's engagements, British gunboats on the Nile had been bombarding Omdurman with lyddite shells, blasting holes in the city's walls and perforating the dome above the Mahdi's tomb. This desecration of their prophet's grave had apparently incensed the Dervishes, igniting their already spirited attacks in the face of such withering rifle fire. When the city fell, the Khalifa had attempted in vain to organise some resistance before praying at his father's tomb and escaping, only to be killed fourteen months later. During the week after the battle, Kitchener ordered that the remains of the Mahdi's tomb be destroyed and his bones be thrown into the Nile. He kept the prophet's skull for himself, transporting it in a paraffin can until he had second thoughts and had it buried secretly in the Muslim cemetery at Wadi Halfa.

To lay the Gordon ghost to rest a memorial service was held outside the old palace in Khartoum. Both the Union Jack and Egyptian flag were raised and Gordon's favourite hymn, 'Abide with Me', was sung while a moved Kitchener sobbed uncontrollably. After the service, Kitchener and Gatacre, among others, searched the ruins for traces of their departed hero.

With the might of the Dervishes destroyed and the death of Gordon avenged, the campaign was effectively over, although Kitchener and a small force continued upstream on a steamer to Fashoda in an attempt to counter French intervention in the Upper Nile region.

In all, Gatacre had done well out of the last eight months, receiving a knighthood, several decorations, and an invitation to dine with Queen Victoria at Windsor Castle. His Aldershot post having been cancelled during his sojourn in the Sudan, he was offered on his return the command of either India's Poona District or England's Eastern District, based in Colchester, and chose the latter, preferring to stay at home after so many years of service overseas. Shortly after assuming his command, he participated in a battle exercise, leading one of the contesting sides to victory using a night march. Clearly fate, with great guile, was already hard at work orchestrating his fall from grace barely a year later.

NINE

Exactly three months after my arrival, the Skemerfontein graves were desecrated. Whoever did it had been very select-ive: neither the Murray nor Barkhuizen graves had been touched, but the marble memorial to the Royal Scots had been shattered and the tombstone of the solitary Cape Police trooper slightly, but tellingly, tampered with. Meti-culously, and in startling contrast to the bludgeoning that the soldiers' memorial must have received, someone using a sharp instrument had removed the capital C from Cape Police. Like a sneering challenge left on a corpse by a psycho-path, this delicate deletion had a peculiar vindictiveness. While the indiscriminate destruction of white graves in an isolated farm cemetery could easily be attributed to a dis-gruntled labourer returning drunk from a party, the presence of so precise an excision suggested something more sinister.

Angus had been alerted by a labourer early on a Monday morning and after inspecting the cemetery himself, had phoned the police and then summoned me and asked my opinion. As we moved through the graves, avoiding the strewn marble fragments and discussing the possibilities, it became clear to both of us that the vandalism was pre-meditated. So close were the oldest Murray graves to the -ape Policeman's that they too would have been damaged had the blows been struck at random. It was clearly, I felt with the inherent vulnerability of a member of a minority group, the act of some Anglophobe. Also, that it had occurred so soon after my arrival suggested that knowledge of my Gatacre study had been a contributory factor. Why else would graves which had rested peacefully for nearly a cen-tury be so suddenly destroyed?

On their arrival, the police made a cursory inspection of the site. A brawny white sergeant, with whom Angus con-versed in Afrikaans, glanced at the mess, asked several rudimentary questions and then announced: 'We must get a dog.' The black constable shadowing him nodded respectfully. The dog, said the sergeant, would arrive that afternoon.

As they drove off, their dusty wake drifting like drizzle across the shearing shed, I reflected on the ironies of a particularly South African situation. Someone desecrates the Anglo-Boer War graves of several British soldiers and a colonial auxiliary on the farm of an English-speaking South African. The police are summoned and an Afrikaner policeman, some members of whose family more than likely suffered at the hands of the British during the war, arrives to investigate. Could he reasonably, given all the enduring divisions and tensions between the two language groups in the country today, be expected to hunt down with diligence a vandal whose actions probably correspond exactly with his own prejudices? The odds are against it. But I may be doing him a disservice. Defying my generalisation, he may be one of those wonderful exceptions who acts contrary to the prescribed prejudices of his own group. At the centre of his creed may be the conviction of equality. I must give him the benefit of the doubt until he condemns himself.

The dog squad arrived after lunch. Comprising a white dog handler with his lean Doberman pinscher bitch and two black constables, they immediately began to scour the cemetery for footprints. Finding that our footprints had obliterated any that the vandal may have left, the handler next led his dog along the outside of the perimeter stone wall, eventually finding several deep imprints in mossy ground alongside a cypress. Stroking and muttering endearments to the bitch, he lowered her head towards each imprint, imploring her gently to smell deeply.

In the meantime the black constables had wandered up the slope to the labourers' cottages where they were talking to several women and children, clearly inveigling them for information. Presently, returning empty-handed, they set off after the handler who was now being led by his dog into the surrounding veld. Angus and I joined the tail of this conga-like procession, following it up a steep, winding track towards the summit of the same long, flat-topped mountain which loomed behind my cottage a kilometre or so to our left. Up we climbed, following the loping, nosing bitch, weaving between the huge boulders that lay scattered across the slope, until we crested the ridge and had the vast panorama of the Stormberg revealed to us.

As we began to cross the grassy plateau, the bitch became curiously animated, scurrying and sniffing and periodically pausing to squat and urinate. The black constables exchanged hopeful glances. Then, inexplicably, she paused and became listless, seemingly having lost the scent. Her handler, obviously used to such lapses, muttered soft words of encouragement which soon restored her animation, propelling her forward among the tussocks with her nose busy. Finding the scent again, she steadied, then began loping briskly with her retinue following closely.

The plateau was divided into three large camps whose boundary fences converged at a common windmill and water trough. Surrounding this central point was a milling mass of sheep through which the bitch cut a swathe. Reaching the trough, and surrounded by the multitude of blank-faced ewes and rams, she again experienced a sudden bout of animation followed closely by lassitude. After sniffing at the spattering of sheep droppings and glancing at her audience, she leaned over the cement brim of the trough, lapped the water and then moved to the windmill and flopped down in its shade. The big blades turning slowly made shadow patterns which raced rhythmically across her shiny coat.

Despite using all his guile, her handler failed to restore her interest. Even when she was led into the grassland beyond the trough in the hope that she would resume her tracking, the bitch showed not the slightest inclination to co-operate. With the spell broken, she became almost coquettish, licking the hands of her handler and wagging the stub of her tail.

It seemed clear to all of us that the desecrator had escaped along that route and had stopped at the trough for a drink. However, the subsequent passage of hundreds of cloven feet had completely erased his scent. Thanks to the woolly hordes he had made good his getaway.

The handler was sympathetic, explaining at length that

although that particular lead had ended, the investigation would continue. Despite his apparent sincerity, I doubted if the mystery of the shattered tombstones would occupy much time among the sleuthing chores of the local police, swamped as they were with stock-theft, house-breaking, arson and murder dockets. After all, only the stones themselves and the dignity of the deceased khakis had suffered any injury. And they were British, and it was long ago.

It took us the remainder of the afternoon to retrace our steps across the plateau and down the mountainside. Throughout the journey the dog padded happily beside us, its tongue lolling. As we neared the sheds, the sun slipped behind Boesmanskop, transforming everything, and in that still half-light that is dusk in that high hinterland, we went our different ways.

TEN

That evening the Roussouws paid me a visit. They arrived just after I had finished my supper, a shy threesome sidling into the sitting-room and settling themselves in a row on the sofa. I offered them a drink and they requested brandies, eschewing the side tables and holding the tumblers in both hands in their laps. At first it was awkward as I probed rather stiltedly in Afrikaans about their sheep and cattle. Koos was their spokesman, replying with canny, homespun truths to the accompaniment of nods from Naas and the old man. As the atmosphere eased, so his answers became longer until sufficient momentum was established for him to pre-empt my next question, pointing at the stack of notes and reference books on the dining-room table.

'I can see that you are working hard on your book.'

'Yes,' I laughed, making light of it, 'I try to work for six hours on most days.'

'Six hours!' he exclaimed, shaking his head, 'your eyes must get very tired.'

I steered the conversation to the war itself, asking for any Boer anecdotes about the immediate environs. 'Pa knows,' said Koos, turning to the old man who lowered his tumbler from his mouth and beamed expectantly. 'Tell Jerry about the time the khakis stole the bread.' Leaning forward on the sofa, Oom Piet Roussouw began to speak:

'One morning the khakis came. It was after the fighting at Boesmansnek and they were looking for the commandos. There was a young lieutenant and about fifteen men. My mother was baking bread. There was just my grandfather, my two brothers, my mother and me. My grandmother was dead and my father was with Commandant Steenkamp at Burgersdorp. The khakis left their horses near the kraal and came to the house. My brothers and I were frightened and clung to my mother's dress. They asked her where my father was. She told them he had been away for months and she didn't know. My mother was a beautiful woman then, with her long black hair tied up on her head, and some of the soldiers said shameful things to her. The lieutenant, who was very young with a red face, told them to keep quiet. He then ordered the house to be searched. When they found nothing, they took the bread and left. Later we found that they had also taken two chickens. My mother always hated the British, especially after my father was killed, but she always spoke well of that young lieutenant.'

I expressed fascination and the old man sipped his brandy, basking in my attention. Naas then interjected in his strange braying voice, reminding his father of the story of the soldier's rock. The old man turned to Koos for approval, and after his nodded consent, began: 'At another time the burghers ambushed the British in the hills near Waggelsdraai. In the hurry to find cover, one khaki could only find a small rock far in front of his comrades. He crouched there like a meer-kat, not daring even to shoot, only twenty feet from the burghers. They shot his rock to pieces but couldn't get him because the other khakis were firing at them from further down the hill. They say that a hundred bullets passed only inches from his body but not one touched him. When British reinforcements arrived, the Boers retreated but the man was frozen there behind the rock. He was so shocked that he couldn't walk. His comrades put him on a horse and led him back to Toomnek. Old Sybrand van Niekerk was there and told me that story.

'But just before the Second World War the man came out here from England with his family. He had been telling them about the rock for years and now that he had sold his business, he had the money to bring them to South Africa to see it. Sybrand took them into the hills behind his house and they found the rock with the grooves of the bullets all over it. When the man saw the rock he started crying. He said his hair had gone white after that day when he had crouched there. Before he left, he gave Sybrand ten pounds to have a drink with any of the other men who had been in that fight. There were a few still living in the district and later they had a big party. While they were drinking, someone took a photo of them on the stoep and later Sybrand wrote greetings on the back of it and sent it to the man in England.'

Naas boomed with laughter; the story's cordial resolution clearly delighted him. On subsiding, he turned towards me, suddenly serious. 'You know, Jerry,' he said, 'I have seen that general of yours.'

'Yes,' interjected the old man animatedly, 'Naas can see strange things.'

'Tell Jerry,' Koos encouraged him. 'Tell him about the day near the sloot.'

Naas wiped a smear of spittle from his chin with his cuff and began a ponderous monologue in his peculiar bray. 'It was late in the morning and we were on our way back home from Toomnek in the bakkie. It was hot and Koos was driving and I was sitting next to him. As we came to the sloot, just down there near Angus Murray's sign (he gestured towards the drawn curtains) we had to stop because the road was full of sheep. They were swarming like bees. Koos drove slowly forward but they wouldn't move out of the way. He had to push them with the bakkie. It was then that I saw the British soldier. He was a thin man with a big moustache and you could see from his face that he was worried. He was in a hurry, pulling and pushing at the sheep, but moving very slowly because they were everywhere. When we passed him he was very close to the window and he looked in at me. I saw that there was dust on his face and patches of sweat on his khaki clothes. I saw also that he had crowns and crossed swords on his shoulders. I knew then that he was Gatacre.'

'Are you sure?' I asked, getting Beatrix's biography and showing him the frontispiece.

'Yes, certain,' he replied, glancing at the photograph, 'that's him.'

'And you saw nothing?' I looked at Koos.

'Nothing. Except the sheep. But they were strange. Something was worrying them. Naas was very excited and when we drove off he asked me if I had seen the soldier. I said "no" and then he told me the story.'

'Did you tell anyone else?'

'We told Pa who said we should tell Hanna Prinsloo, there behind Fluistervlakte. Hanna is a bit mad but very clever. We told her but she said she didn't know what the story meant.'

As the conversation continued, I made a mental note of Naas's account, repeating it to myself in the smallest detail, wondering how it could be included in my biography. The presence of the sheep was particularly interesting. The more I researched Gatacre, the more his destiny seemed linked to the dumb animals.

Nothing else of consequence was discussed that evening. We abandoned history and continued with trivia. Later I offered them coffee and rusks and they accompanied me to the kitchen and we talked while the kettle boiled. At one point while we sat crunching, the conversation briefly suspended, I found myself wondering whether these three men had anything to do with the desecration of the graves. Confronted, the very idea seemed ludicrous, so I quickly dismissed it. Whatever their failings, I told myself, there was nothing devious about the Roussouws. To endorse my stand, they were suitably outraged when I told them about it. Koos shook his head. 'Nobody,' he said, 'but an idiot would meddle with the dead. Not even a kaffir.'

It was nearly midnight when they left. I accompanied them to their bakkie. It was a clear night and a breeze was hushing the pines. Far in the distance towards Boesmansnek a light popped on, then off, then on again — a car, probably, negotiating the bends of the pass.

The following day I learnt from Angus that from time to time the Roussouws arrived unannounced on his doorstep after dark and stayed and drank and watched television until the stations closed. He had, he said, always attempted to be accommodating; they were good neighbours, monitoring his flocks behind the mountain and alerting him if an animal was in distress. Also, that they were simple folk on the periphery of their own Afrikaans society made them friends worth fostering. Without strong tribal loyalties, they weren't Anglophobic although in their guileless simplicity they often denigrated liberal, urban English-speakers in his presence, seemingly oblivious of his own Englishness and political preference. The fact that he was merely from a prominent farming family long established in the Stormberg seemed somehow to exclude him from censure.

It was always a mystery to me why three Afrikaners who found the Nationalist government treacherously left-wing coveted the friendship of English-speaking liberals like Angus and myself. Angus, however, professed to have solved the riddle over the years. The Roussouws' company, he felt, wasn't sought by fellow Afrikaners because in their simplicity, the quaint threesome were bywoner throwbacks. While they may have had much in common with the anachronistic inhabitants of Fluistervlakte — a quaint hamlet tucked away in the mountains not far from Skemerfontein — they were far removed from the more established Afrikaner farmers who were attempting to escape from the very memories that the presence of the Roussouws rekindled.

ELEVEN

Illustrated diagrammatically, and with some licence, my sojourn in the Stormberg resembled a long-stemmed flower. With my journey to Skemerfontein tracing one side of the stem's outline and my return to Natal the other, my movements on the farm and within the vicinity of Toomnek created by pointillism the face of the bloom, and my frequent excursions beyond my immediate surroundings (to the battlefield, Fluistervlakte, De Montmorency's death-place and Olive Schreiner's grave, among others) formed the fringe of soft serrations. Across the uniformity of the pincushion face, however, appeared two slight mutations: a pair of very different stripes, each radiating outwards from the centre. One was a seam of bolder, more lustrous colour stitched by the vitality of my relationship with Katie, while the other, diametrically opposite and resembling a cicatrix, denoted the episode of the fugitive and the ensuing tragedy. Stretching my credulity somewhat, I linked my year-long stay to that rather ridiculous totem, tacking each new occurrence somewhere on the anatomy of the bloom.

My first meeting with Katie, and therefore the first real stitches of the vivid seam, took place at a dinner party at the Murrays early in autumn. She had returned the previous day for a university holiday and the party was a homecoming celebration. As Andrew had gone fishing in Natal with friends, there were only six of us: the three Murrays, the Thorntons (a couple, old friends of the family, who farmed closer to Toomnek) and myself, the tenant and aspirant biographer.

After bathing and dressing up somewhat in a pair of smartish trousers and a sports jacket, I strolled down the hillside as the dusk became darkness, carrying a torch and a bellyful of butterflies at the possibility of botching my first meeting with the girl who looked so wonderful in the family photograph on Angus's desk. As I neared the homestead, Jess, the Murrays' border collie, bounded out from her kennel beside the kitchen door, barking initially but then subsiding into a nuzzled welcome when she recognised the figure which she had encountered so often wandering around her domain. I patted her briefly before several tiny movements in a bed of chrysanthemums pulled her away, transforming her into a bounding piebald shape, all nose and alertness.

The garden between the homestead and the base of the hillside had been formally arranged by Mary into a fan of rectangular rose beds and I remember thinking that evening how the nearest pink effusion resembled a dormitory of sleeping flamingoes. That the image — each standard rose with its long stem emulated a sleeping bird poised on one leg with its head lost in a canopy of pinkness — has remained clear is because it was briefly the foreground of my first glimpse of Katie.

She was seated on the sill of the bay window in Angus's study and with the curtains undrawn I could see her profile clearly in the warm light which diffused from somewhere deeper in the room. Standing motionless, merging with the foliage as Jess snuffled beside me, I watched as Katie spoke animatedly to someone whose gesticulations presumably caused the shadows which danced periodically across her face. Initially, the tempo of the patterns seemed too animated to reflect the movements of someone as phlegmatic as Angus but, as I soon discovered, it was only in his daughter's company that he discarded his natural reserve. With her, at times, he was almost ebullient. There had always, said Katie later, been a vibrancy in their relationship, one in which two essentially placid natures bubbled and sallied with an endless stream of mutually interesting ideas. Memories, art, history, sheep, politics — each raced after the other, punctuated on that occasion from my darkening perspective among the flowers only by bursts of laughter, during which Katie flung her head backwards and her longish auburn hair flounced over the cream blouse she was wearing. Beaded by the window frame, warmed by the interior light, and framed, from my perspective, by the darkness of the garden, the image she formed was indelible.

Apprehensive, but more eager still, I abandoned my refuge and strode to the side door, knocked and before anyone had time to respond, stepped inside. Accompanied only by the benign creaking of the old floorboards, I suppressed my apprehension and headed for the study and the voices and laughter that emanated from it.

While I foolishly expected the impact of our meeting to be remarkable, it wasn't. Like countless others it was merely cordial and formal; no more. Katie, who was speaking when I entered, paused on seeing me and Angus quickly filled the void with a cheery greeting and introduction. Still poised on the sill, her long legs crossed and dangling, Katie said 'Hello Jeremy' and extended a hand which I shook with what I considered was the correct combination of firmness and limpness.

'I've just been telling Katie about you,' said Angus and laughed his quiet laugh.

'Nice things, I hope,' I said awkwardly.

'Of course,' he laughed again. 'Come, let's go through.'

Katie slid from the sill and we followed her past the stuffed korhaan and a set of Finch-Davies prints into the passage. It was then that I first remember noting her stylishness. The cream blouse and magenta skirt patterned with intricate African motifs were different, being neither prissily bourgeois nor trendily ethnic as the blouse or skirt, taken separately, may have suggested.

Mary met us in the sitting-room and while Angus was at the cellarette pouring drinks, a flurry of barks from Jess heralded the Thorntons' arrival. A couple who were of similar age to Angus and Mary, the Thorntons too were prominent farmers long established in the district. Harold was slight with a ruddy complexion scarred by pale blotches where outbreaks of skin cancer had been surgically removed, the result of a fair skin exposed for decades to an unrestrained sun. Contrastingly, his wife Joan had a flawless complexion, pale as alabaster and without the tinge of swarthiness which usually characterises such resilience. The juxtaposition was striking and, as if sensing my reaction, Mary produced a photo album after the Thorntons had left, indicating a snapshot of four young adults at a picnic. It was the Murrays and the Thorntons taken three decades previously. All were bare-headed and Harold's face showed no sign of the tumours that were later to disfigure him.

'His skin was fine then,' said Mary, pointing. 'It's terrible what the sun can do.'

Recalling her reaction, here in this cottage within sight and sound of the sea, reminds me of Gatacre's troops sweltering in the train trucks on the day before the battle, their fair skins searing in the sun. Clearly, some things haven't changed. As the sun roasted the Tommies, so it still roasts all of us with pallid skins. Examples like Harold Thornton have scared me into prudence. My army bush hat became an appendage during that year whenever it was sunny. Now, embalmed by humidity, I can be more reckless, but at my peril still.

For the purposes of this story, what was memorable about that evening wasn't only my unremarkable but significant meeting with Katie, but the first glimpse of someone else. And, unbeknown to him, Harold Thornton performed the introduction. Wanting to hear the weather report for some agricultural reason, he put on the television, catching the tail-end of the news. I remember ignoring the low-pitched intrusion and continuing my conversation with Katie, exchanging news about university. My two years of medical studies having admitted me to that smallish fraternity of English-speaking students, we had several mutual acquaintances to discuss and it was while we were thus engrossed that the news reader caught our attention.

Displaying a mug shot of a black youth during the repeat of the news headlines, the voice-over described him as one Elias Mbuyembu, wanted by the police in connection with a bomb blast in East London the previous week which had killed an elderly woman and two teenage girls. Next followed a physical description — height, build, complexion, distinguishing features, some of which I remember — and the warning that he was highly dangerous and shouldn't be confronted. Instead, cautioned the report, contact a number that flashed briefly on the screen or your local police station.

'Good God,' said Harold as the portrait vanished and the news-readers said their good-nights. 'That fellow Mbuyembu used to work for us. Remember, Joanie, the chap who burnt his hand with the welder.'

'Oh yes,' she replied, 'the one who fixed the trellis in the garden.'

'He was a bright blighter,' Harold continued. 'He could fix anything — tractors, irrigation equipment. He once completely rebuilt a chaff-cutter after they'd made a mess of it in Toomnek. And he was an abstemious chap. Never smoked. Whenever we were out on the lands and stopped for a smoke break and all the others lit up, he would just sit and chat. He was a bachelor. Bloody good worker. Used to look after himself and was in good shape and never hung over on Mondays like the others.'

'What became of him?' asked Mary.

'I don't know. One day he just disappeared. The other chaps said he had gone to East London. They gave me an address to send his pay to but I never heard if he got it.'

'Off to join the struggle,' said Katie pointedly.

'God, you'd never have thought so,' said Harold, 'he seemed such a sensible fellow.'

And that was all I heard of Elias Mbuyembu for several months. But, alas, not for ever. He was soon to play a pivotal role in my life, so much so that it seemed as if a string of coincidences had conjured our meeting that evening. Had Katie not arrived home the previous day, had the Thorntons not been old friends and consequently invited to the get-together, had Harold not wanted to see the weather report, Mbuyembu would not have entered my life until several months later, if (coincidences again) at all.

Supper followed shortly afterwards and the incident receded, its prominence usurped by a round of beef, a smooth pinotage and the general conviviality. I sat beside Katie and remember relishing the smell of her, something which I now take for granted. We were all at the table for several hours, our ready dialogue soon becoming a dynamo that fired its own momentum, and as the evening passed so my observation of it has faded. One fragment, however, I do remember. It was Harold Thornton's voice and he was asking Angus whether the police had made any headway in the case of the desecrated graves.

'No,' said Angus, compressing tobacco in his pipe with a finger, 'nothing that we know of.'

'It seems pretty fishy to me,' Harold continued. 'I think it's some Afrikaner being vindictive because Jeremy's research has opened up old wounds.'

'But surely no one still bears that much of a grudge?' I asked.

'God, you don't know some of those fellows,' countered Harold. 'Especially those out towards Fluistervlakte. They're as inbred as meerkats. One of them could have got a bee in his bonnet and cut across the veld one night with a four-pound hammer and a chisel.'

'To achieve what?' I asked.

'God knows. To put the wind up your sails and Angus's as your landlord. Many of them lost relatives in the Boer War and they still hate our guts. Why they can't put it behind them, I don't know. My uncle was killed with the South African Light Horse at Spioenkop but I don't blame every Afrikaner I meet for his death. Their Anglophobia is some sort of rallying point. Uniting against the common enemy, like this "total onslaught" tripe.'

Katie was listening and from across the table I saw Joan glance at Harold and give Mary a long-suffering look as if what he was saying was an old hobby-horse which she had heard many times before.

'Ah, it's all a bit of a mystery,' said Angus thoughtfully, pipe in hand. 'Let's have a nightcap.'

It was after midnight before we began leaving. The Thorntons offered to drive me home but the thought of Harold negotiating the narrow track up the hillside made me decline politely under the guise of wanting to walk and clear my head. Not long after their car eased down the driveway, its tail-lights flickering beyond the long-legged roses, I set off up the slope, weaving through the darkness, being led by the small, bobbing hologram which my torch cast ahead of me. The chillness did soon clear my senses and I reached the cottage jubilant at having met Katie at last. Whenever I tell her now of my jubilation that evening, and that I have written it into my Skemerfontein story, she laughs ambiguously and kisses me lightly on the lips.

TWELVE

My first outing with Katie was a pilgrimage to Olive Schreiner's tomb. Long an admirer of the indomitable feminist, Katie had noticed *The Story of an African Farm* among my historical reference books and had suggested the visit. Having just read and enjoyed the novel, and being at that stage in my relationship with Katie when I wanted nothing more than to be with her and to please her, I took little coaxing. Driving down from my cottage before dawn the following day, I stopped at the main house where we had a cup of coffee and then set out, gliding slowly down the driveway, with sheep in the adjoining paddock moving through poplars in the mist like bent woodgatherers in woolly clothing.

The journey to Cradock took several hours. Arriving mid-morning in a haze of heat, we drove through the town with its imposing Dutch Reformed church — a replica of St Martin's-in-the-Fields — and crossed the Fish River. Then, with Katie navigating, we bore south-eastwards along the river's southern bank in the direction of Halesowen, a railway siding on the line between Cradock and Cookhouse. Unsure of our bearings, we stopped on several occasions to ask directions from black pedestrians but none of them had heard of Olive Schreiner or knew of the whereabouts of a white person's grave in the vicinity.

Stopping at the railway siding itself, we found the toothless station-master in a hut and asked him directions. He said he knew nothing of the area, having arrived only the previous week. Neither had he heard of Olive Schreiner. He shouted in Afrikaans for his coloured assistant, his crimped lips pouting momentarily before subsiding again. Presently a man appeared and ambled towards us, his heavy boots crunching on the gravel.

'Do you know the grave of Olive . . .?' began the station-master in Afrikaans and then paused and turned to me.

'Schreiner,' I said.

'Skreiner,' he repeated.

'Yes, it's up there,' said the assistant, pointing at a koppie that loomed in the distance behind the hut. 'You must drive on until the tar ends and then look on your right for a gate. That's the farm where the grave is.'

We found the gate without difficulty. Crossing the railway line and passing beneath the sign and a buffalo skull and horns, we drove slowly along a rutted track through the thorn trees until we reached a dusty farmyard festooned with drying goat skins and centred by a large tractor on bricks. Seeing us arrive, a young man appeared from a small house beside which was a windmill which groaned as it attempted to keep what breeze there was in its face. We exchanged greetings and, drawing yet again on my rather crude Afrikaans, slightly honed after two years of national service, I asked him if we could visit Olive Schreiner's grave.

'Yes,' he said, 'sure. Come, I'll show you where it is.'

We crossed to a track which led behind the house and past a squabble of outbuildings and labourers' huts. Pointing at a distant koppie whose steep sides distinguished it from the others, he warned: 'There's Buffelskop. The grave's on top. But it's far, and it's hot.' Then, after a pause he added: 'Shall I get a boy to show you?'

'Don't worry, thank you,' I said. 'We won't get lost.'

'No,' he laughed. 'You won't get lost, but you'll get tired.'

We set off slowly, skirting the outbuildings and huts, following a rutted track across a dry watercourse and towards the towering conical shape. The veld was ochre-coloured and, unlike Skemerfontein, devoid of grass. Only the Karoo bushes and occasional dwarfish trees seemed to have the necessary tenacity to survive. Pointing at the bushes as we bumped and weaved, dust tumbling behind us, Katie exclaimed: 'They look like pot scourers.' Which they did, with all their squatness and brittleness.

After a quarter of an hour of painstaking progress, we reached the foot of the koppie. Parking the bakkie, we clambered out and began our ascent. Lumbered by a rucksack containing refreshments and a camera, I led the way up the steep incline, repeatedly pitching forward onto all fours when the loose shale slid from under me. Protesting that my landslides were making her progress impossible, Katie soon asked if she could lead the way. I readily agreed and the sight of her haunches heaving above me was a welcome diversion until fatigue drained all energy for salaciousness. Thereafter, everything became our painstaking quest for the summit which seemed no closer whenever we paused for breath and looked up at it.

Eventually, we reached the rocky knoll, two thousand feet above the plain, and clambered between ironstone boulders to the summit itself. There, on a morgen of rocky ground strewn with Karoo bushes and several stunted trees whose proportions suggested bonsai experiments long abandoned, was the sarcophagus, a small granite igloo. Crossing to it, we found a brass plate listing its occupants:

OLIVE SCHREINER
CRONWRIGHT-SCHREINER
BABY
AND 'NITA'

As we stood there, side by side, it seemed incredible that entombed with her husband, infant daughter and favourite dog on that isolated eyrie was Olive Schreiner herself. That there, far from the glitter of city life often associated with English speakers in South Africa, was the novelist who first gave that portion of this southern subcontinent a voice in the English language. And yet, as we stood there, our forearms touching but our hands unclasped, like lovers in church, it began to seem more and more fitting that the creator of *The Story of an African Farm* was where she belonged, surrounded by the landscape that provided both her raw material and the setting for the halcyon early days of her marriage before the prolonged separations.

I found myself moved by her simple tomb as I had been by the graves of the soldiers in the Skemerfontein cemetery, and yet more so because she really belonged and wasn't merely the residue of Empire. Katie professes that she was similarly moved. Olive Schreiner's presence was an affirmation of our own existence so far from our origins. With her there on the koppie we had a placebo with which to allay our uncertainties. No matter what the future held in store, we both thought, Olive Schreiner had opted to stay and that was good enough for us.

Finding a rosette of shade beneath one of the stunted trees, we sat down and drank from an army water-bottle and ate biscuits. While we rested, a brisk breeze frisked the scant foliage around us, enlivening the dust into scurries but doing little to counter the searing heat. Far in the distance the roofs of Cradock could be seen, glinting like lost jewellery in the ochre vastness.

'Take all that,' said Katie suddenly, indicating the endless barren plain below us, 'and superimpose on it the occasional white homestead — that is the subject of my Master's thesis. I'll tell you about it sometime. But let's rest now.'

Lying down beside each other, we had a nap before taking several photographs, each capturing the other beside the igloo, our faces sheened with sweat and our damp hair plastered to our heads by our hats. Then we said goodbye to the entombed and Buffelskop and began the steep descent.

On our way out we stopped at the house to thank the farmer but he wasn't there. We headed back past Halesowen to Cradock and thence, via Tarkastad, Queenstown and Toomnek, to Skemerfontein. En route I found myself pondering on the durability of Olive Schreiner's grave. Far more than its inaccessibility and solidity, her memory was its best custodian. Unlike the khakis' graves, hers wasn't tainted by imperialism. Lovers of her books aside, nobody could find fault with her multiracial humanitarianism. Consequently, no one should feel compelled to desecrate her memorial. No reasonable person, that is.

It was dark when we turned in at the familiar gate with its merino ram sign. Katie invited me to supper and we spoke animatedly about Olive Schreiner and the tomb. Mary and Angus had visited Buffelskop a decade previously and had felt similar emotions. Angus likened Olive Schreiner's desire to be buried there to his own family's wish to end up in the Skemerfontein cemetery. Everyone should be buried, we resolved unanimously, where they felt they belonged.

Rising suddenly from the table, Angus disappeared in the direction of his study and, after several minutes, returned with an open book in his hand.

'Listen to this,' he said quietly, and began reading, his voice like a prow slicing through the silence.

'They throw in Drummer Hodge, to rest
Uncoffined — just as found:
His landmark is a kopje-crest
That breaks the veldt around;
And foreign constellations west
Each night above his mound.

'Young Hodge the Drummer never knew —
Fresh from his Wessex home —
The meaning of the broad Karoo,
The bush, the dusty loam,
And why uprose to nightly view
Strange stars amid the gloam.

'Yet portion of that unknown plain
Will Hodge for ever be;
His homely Northern breast and brain
Grow to some Southern tree,
And strange-eyed constellations reign
His stars eternally.

'Thomas Hardy's *Drummer Hodge*,' said Angus on ending. 'Sad, isn't it?' He then sat down, placing the book on the table beside him.

'Yes,' said Katie, 'he's like those soldiers in the sloot.'

After supper we moved to the sitting-room for coffee and our discussion shifted to Katie's art studies and the subject of her Master's thesis. After much thought, she said, she had decided on the bywoner community at Fluistervlakte. She would paint and interview them in an attempt to portray

82

a white community that had become truly African. They hadn't merely gone native, she said; they had been native for generations.

Later, when I got up to leave, she followed me outside to the bakkie. As we stood talking in the darkness, she asked me whether I would accompany her to Fluistervlakte later in the week. 'All right,' I said, jumping at her offer but tempering my response.

We then embraced and kissed and I ran my hands down her sides as if gently frisking her, tracing the curve of her hips. Although our necking soon filled us with passion, consummation came only several days later, on my bed in the cottage with the doves crooning on the ledges and the wind moaning in the pines. That evening, after our Schreiner visit and Angus's recitation, I left Katie reluctantly and drove off through the dark yard and up the hillside. The moon was waning and the mountain behind my cottage looked huge and dark beside the low sweep of the valley.

THIRTEEN

To call Fluistervlakte a hamlet would be an exaggeration. It was nothing more than a church, police station, general dealer and about fifteen cottages scattered across a grassy slope. There was neither a main street nor electricity, and none of the roads was tarred. Unlike Toomnek, it had no cohesion of its own; the simple cottages were dotted haphazardly on the grasslands. Established late last century by a group of Dutch Reformed Church parishioners disenchanted with their dominee in Toomnek, its choice of location stemmed more from a need to be just outside the boundaries of the Toomnek parish than from the actual suitability of the site. Plagued by its inaccessibility and an erratic water supply, Fluistervlakte never burgeoned into the alternative community it was intended to become and within decades all but the most fervent dissenters had abandoned it.

When Katie and I visited the community over a century after its founding, half of its cottages were deserted and none of its white inhabitants, bar two young constables in the police station, was under fifty years old. Hidden among the hills some thirty kilometres from Skemerfontein, it was as much a nineteenth century relic as one could hope to find in contemporary South Africa.

Katie's plan of action was simple: she would explain to each person whom we approached that for her university studies she needed to paint portraits. For her subjects, she would continue, she had chosen the people of the Stormberg because she too was from the region. As her method of painting involved days of work in her studio, she would need to take photographs of her subjects for later reference. However, as the university authorities wanted more than just paintings, she also needed some background information on each person. This necessitated a number of questions.

She hoped they wouldn't mind the intrusion? With only one exception, they didn't.

Most of her questions were sufficiently impersonal to avoid accusations of prying, although that was essentially what she was doing. 'Are you worried about the troubles in the townships?' she would venture with sufficient levity to lessen the chance of defensiveness. 'You know, there are certain areas inside the country where even the army doesn't go unless the soldiers are well-armed and in Buffels. Do you think things will get worse? Are you worried about your safety? Do you feel that you'll be able to live as peacefully as this forever, or do you think that the troubles will one day reach Fluistervlakte?' Thus, in tones of gentle cajolery and in fluent Afrikaans, Katie managed to extract opinions and even confidences from her interviewees. Hovering in the background, I would unobtrusively note each person's response, watching as Katie constructed a picture of the community in a manner not unlike my attempts to conjure up Gatacre.

The first cottage we visited was small and ramshackle. Despite its dilapidation, however, the precise construction of its stone walls harked back to a masonic excellence extremely rare today. Abutting one of its walls was a chicken-run: an untidy tangle of wire netting and corrugated-iron within which several lean Leghorns were scuffing and pecking. As we approached the verandah a mongrel tethered to a peach tree began yapping wildly, and from the hen-house emerged an elderly man with a slouch hat and an enamel bowl containing eggs. His face was wizened and the white stubble of his beard resembled spilled sugar and contrasted sharply with the darkness of his complexion.

We introduced ourselves and then Katie gave her spiel. Daan Fourie listened attentively, nodding from time to time. When she had finished, he paused briefly, absently stroking one of the eggs, before agreeing. As Katie positioned him within the dappled shade of the peach, snapping photographs and nattering, I remember noting that his cottage had a humbleness not usually associated with whites' dwelling places in South Africa. Despite its solidity and the quality of its masonry, the black labourers' cottages on Skemerfontein were superior. Daan Fourie, I remember jolting myself, was a 'poor white', one of that predominantly Afrikaner phenomenon spawned by British domination, drought, inbreeding, bad farming methods and the whole gamut of afflictions associated with socio-economic deprivation. Unlike the Roussouws, who lived in similar circumstances, he had no land, bar the patch around his house. What made him an anachronism, though, was that despite the Nationalist government's determined efforts to eradicate poverty among its volk, he and many of the other inhabitants of Fluistervlakte had somehow missed the benefits.

When it came to his interrogation, Katie's questions about the endemic violence in the country's townships and the possibility of ripples into such tranquil inlets as Fluistervlakte met with a disconcerting blankness. While Daan Fourie had heard of the troubles on his radio, he didn't know where the particular hot spots were. The police, he was sure, would handle it. Unrest would never come to Fluistervlakte. He knew because he had lived there all his life. The government wouldn't allow it. Anyway, he didn't think much about such things.

That the police had for the previous year been unable to contain the insurrection without assistance, and that the use of troops for township control was now a feature of South African life, had missed him. Of all the internecine violence, the butchering and pillage, he had only the vaguest inkling. His limited curiosity had little room for doom-laden thoughts. He lived a solitary life and that portion of his mind that wasn't blank was occupied by his immediate needs and his dog and chickens. Further than that he knew nothing of the outside world.

We thanked him and moved on. The next house was deserted, its window panes broken and its door creaking on its hinges. Twists of excrement were visible on the faded linoleum and scratched on an inner wall in a childish hand were the words: 'Moer die Boere'. Outside was a rusted water tank encased in a lattice of contorted vines. Taking a footpath through the grass we found another house locked and barred and also apparently deserted. Peering through grubby lace curtains we saw a deal table, several chairs and an anthracite heater beneath a row of kitsch religious pictures. Unlike its predecessor whose fate was obviously sealed, this house seemed to be resisting dereliction. Although teetering on the brink, it was holding out.

Our next encounter awaited us across an expanse of grassland. Leaning on a cattle gate, Hendrik and Santie Vosloo greeted us expansively as we approached and ushered us towards their house, even before Katie could explain our motives. Both had fine faces, deeply lined after decades of exposure to the harsh elements. They also had that refreshing receptiveness — or naivety perhaps — common among some country folk that precluded the need for strained introductions. Once we knew each other's names, we were friends of long standing. Santie shouted to a maid to make coffee and we were settled on chairs on the verandah. When Katie requested their cooperation in her project, they were delighted by the idea.

'Once we have drunk our coffee,' said Hendrik, 'you can take the photos. But now we must talk.'

They had, Hendrik explained, only lived in Fluistervlakte for five years. Before that their life had been hard. As a young man he had inherited a barren, rocky farm and for thirty years he and Santie had wrested a meagre living from it. They had educated their children well but not without great sacrifice. When their son finally decided on a life in the city, they had sold the farm and moved to Fluistervlakte. Although it was sad to have lost their land, they now had no worries and could spend their last days in peace and modest comfort.

'Look,' said Hendrik, pointing northwards to a range of hills, 'that krantz with the sun shining on it, where those cattle are grazing, that's on our farm. Sometimes I just sit here and watch it and remember.' We gazed out across the grassland, the roofs of several cottages and the radio aerial towering above the police station to the distant precipice sheened in silver by the afternoon sun.

'What,' Katie began gingerly, 'do you think of the trouble

87

in the townships?' Before the Vosloos could answer, she elaborated on her question, relating the violence both to the country at large and specifically to the Fluistervlakte community. Not wanting to give the rather sinister impression of an outsider bent merely on inveigling political opinions from strangers, she explained at length why she needed the information. The true nature of the person and their relationship to their environment, and their views on the future, were crucial to substantiate her portraits. Hence the questions.

'What Santie and I hear on the radio frightens us,' began Hendrik, turning to Santie for affirmation and getting a sombre nod. 'We don't have TV so we don't see the pictures but every day we hear on the radio that people are being killed. People are often killed in fighting but not day after day for years. The fighting has become normal now. People have forgotten how life was before it started.'

'But surely the reason's politics?' ventured Katie tentatively. 'That's why it doesn't stop.'

The arrival of the coffee and the distribution of cups delayed Hendrik's reply but presently he began, to the accompaniment of Santie's offer of rusks. 'Yes,' he said, stirring his coffee, 'but it's really history. Us whites are caught by history. We are a small people in Africa who are surrounded. Our choice is simple: either we fight or we die. So far we are fighting; that's why the soldiers are in the townships. But we are not fighting hard enough. That's why the fighting never stops. When a rooikat is cornered, it doesn't attack only those hunters who are holding guns; it attacks everyone. That's what we must do. If there's trouble we must bomb the townships and make everyone suffer and not waste our time just searching for the troublemakers. It needs a total-war policy like the British taught us in the Anglo-Boer War. When they couldn't win on the battlefield, they destroyed the farms and locked up the women and children. Many died, as you know. My grandmother and two of my mother's sisters died at Brandfort. We must do the same to the kaffirs. It's terrible, I know, but there is no justice in Africa. Once we are down no one will help us up again.'

'But will that solve the problem?' asked Katie.

'No,' said Santie, 'it won't solve the problem. But we have no choice.' A plump tabby, curled up on her lap, stretched and began preening itself.

The remainder of our conversation centred around the ethics and implications of Hendrik's 'total-war policy'. Maintaining as best she could a position of impartiality, Katie probed and parried. In essence, it seemed that Hendrik was advocating what he saw as the lesser evil: to die fighting rather than to capitulate and face the consequences. Of this both he and Santie were adamant, and bolstered by their conviction they faced the future with grim confidence.

Our next encounter was short. Dawie Moolman, whom Hendrik had recommended as canny but cantankerous, lived some distance from the other cottages. An erudite recluse who regularly borrowed books from the Toomnek library, he was, said the Vosloos, Fluistervlakte's sage. Anyone with a problem sought Moolman's advice. A worldly man with a reputedly colourful past, his wisdom cut through uncertainties — to use Hendrik's simile — like a panga through a pumpkin.

After a five-minute walk through the gently swaying grass, we found Moolman outside his cottage sharpening a cut-throat razor on a strop suspended from the branch of a pine tree. He was a large, heavy man wearing baggy khakis and a grubby cardigan and he drew the blade across the leather in long rhythmical strokes. On reaching his gate, we greeted him. Without replying, he hesitated and swivelled slowly to face us. Prompted by the awkward silence, Katie began her explanation and Moolman appeared to listen attentively, a lumbering figure with the bright blade of the razor in his hand. When Katie had finished, there was silence again. In the hope of generating a response, I mentioned that everything would take only a few minutes. Slowly, Moolman shifted his gaze from Katie to me and back to Katie again. Then, suddenly and quite unbidden, he bellowed 'Fuck off', turned his back on us and resumed his sharpening. Momentarily benumbed, we hesitated, conscious only of the slow slap-scrape of the blade along the strop, before retreating.

It was now late afternoon and the descent of the sun behind the church and its windbreak of cedars had allowed the first chill of evening to emerge. Woodsmoke, curling up into the quiet clearness from several cottage chimneys, was pleasantly aromatic as we returned slightly shaken to the bakkie. Deciding to call it a day, we drove back along the dusty road past the police station. As we turned left at the trading store and accelerated for the district road, we passed a cottage in whose yard an obese old white woman in a wheelchair was being pushed by an emaciated and equally elderly black woman. I braked and quite unashamedly we watched as the frail attendant, wearing a shapeless floral dress and checked slippers, struggled to propel her mistress up a ramp onto the verandah. Swathed in a Basuto blanket from which only her jowled face protruded, the passenger appeared to be muttering instructions as her nodding attendant laboured. This spectacle of black frailty serving white obesity would have rolled unaided into a Gillray caricature, entitled 'Exploitation' perhaps, or 'Gluttony Wheeled By Want'. At a time when the tables were turning, such an anachronism had to be captured.

Both participants had been inside several minutes before we knocked on the front door. Presently, silhouetted by lamplight, the maid reappeared.

'Could we speak to the missus?' Katie asked.

'Yes,' she replied.

We followed her inside to a small shuttered living room with several chairs and a table. Cocooned in her blanket, the old woman was wedged in an armchair, staring at the glowing coals of a fire. She looked up as we entered and her eyes were bright and beady in the lamplight. Once again Katie explained everything.

'Where do you come from?' the old woman interrupted in Afrikaans.

'A farm near Toomnek,' said Katie.

'Are you going home now?'

'Yes.'

'Then you must watch out for kaffirs. It's dangerous for a woman to travel alone on these roads.'

'I'm driving with my friend,' said Katie, gesturing in my direction.

'Good,' said the old woman, the light from the lamp and fire alternately hardening and softening her heavy features as she nodded. 'Because if the kaffirs are standing across the road, you mustn't stop, you must drive through them.'

If anyone could be said to live in mortal fear of blacks, it was Anna Strydom. As the remainder of our conversation revealed, she lived in a continual state of anxiety. All blacks were menacing, whether they were itinerants requesting work in the garden, kwedins begging for sweets at the trading store or travellers queuing at the crossroads for the railway bus. None could be trusted. Foremost in their minds were robbery, rape and murder. No white should take any chances. Katie's questions about the township violence and its consequences for Fluistervlakte received the stock replies of a paranoid racist. Her fear destroyed all reason. No blacks were good.

What was particularly bizarre about Anna Strydom was that she made no allowance for Maria Vikazi, her black attendant on whom she was totally dependent. While she vilified blacks with such venom, inscrutable Maria stood at her shoulder smiling. Unable to question her alone, we never found out her feelings. Was her hatred suppressed by necessity or had years of abuse established a greater tolerance? We suspected the former.

No allowance was made for our attitudes which, had Anna Strydom been even remotely perceptive, she should have construed as liberal and therefore at odds with her own. It seemed that our whiteness was all that mattered. We were united in our fight for survival. That other whites could hold contrary opinions was somehow beyond her comprehension.

The photo session which followed was a great success. Looking like an amalgam of Queen Victoria and President Kruger in old age, Anna Strydom peered grimly from her blanket as Katie snapped her from different angles. The results proved to be striking: veneered by the lamplight and the glow from the fire, the portraits emphasised the pallor and lined podginess of the old woman's face. Any fresh observer would vouch for the indomitability of the subject,

91

but Katie and I, with the hindsight of her answers, could detect the hollowness behind the gruff facade.

It was dusk when we left Fluistervlakte. The wide gravel road climbed gradually to a rocky ridge and then descended sharply onto an open plain. As we sped along in the twilight, with the dust billowing behind us and the empty vastness stretching endlessly into the distance, Katie spoke excitedly about having the photographs developed and beginning the portraits. Then, saying that she was exhausted, she leaned over and placed her head on my shoulder. It was snug in the bakkie and her hair was soft and fragrant. As I sat relishing her closeness and watching the headlights probe the settling darkness, it occurred to me that although only thirty kilometres separated Fluistervlakte and Skemerfontein, they were in fact a century apart. Katie and I were time travellers in a capsule with the telephone poles flashing past like years.

FOURTEEN

Early in October 1899, in anticipation of an outbreak of hostilities between Britain and the Boer republics, Gatacre was informed that he had been given the command of the Third Infantry Division of the Army Corps in South Africa. A fortnight later, with war now declared, he boarded, to great applause from a large crowd, the Union Castle Line mail steamer *Moor* with his associates, Lieutenants General Lord Methuen and Sir Francis Clery, commanders of the First and Second Infantry Divisions respectively.

The journey to the battlefront is a frustrating time for eager soldiers and one can picture the trio pacing the deck together — the tall and walrus-moustached Methuen, the brawny and bewhiskered Clery and the lean and restless Gatacre — discussing points of strategy, planning, their deliberations charged with the expectancy of action. Methuen, however, thought that the war would be over before their arrival and ribbed Gatacre for diligently typing memos for his staff as the steamer ploughed southwards. That Gatacre felt otherwise was revealed during the embarkation at Southampton when a lady onlooker expressed similar doubts to Methuen's about the duration of the war. 'Make no mistake,' Gatacre had replied gravely, 'we have a long tough job ahead of us.' Although essentially correct, we can with hindsight detect the ambiguity of his statement: Britain had a long, tough job ahead but he himself would be back home in seven months with his career shattered.

On his arrival at Cape Town, General Sir Redvers Buller, the Commander-in-Chief, found a deteriorating situation with Kimberley and Ladysmith beleaguered. Sending Methuen and the First Division to rescue the diamond diggings, he decided to set out for Natal himself, taking with him Clery's Second Division and two brigades from Gatacre's Third Division. Thus emasculated, Gatacre and his single remaining battalion were despatched to the Eastern Cape with orders to hold Queenstown if possible and East London at all costs and to stem the tide of invasion and rebellion.

Confronted by the increasing danger of widespread disaffection and inundated with requests for protection from Dutch and English loyalists, Gatacre could do nothing, having insufficient troops either to provide assistance or to strike the sudden and decisive blow that was so desperately needed. For all commanders such a predicament would have been extremely trying but for Gatacre, who breathed action, it was doubly so. However, after the arrival of reinforcements late in November, he was able to advance from Queenstown to Putterskraal, bolster his forward posts at Boesmanshoek and Penhoek on the Stormberg range and wait until the arrival of yet more troops early in December allowed him to begin his offensive. A letter written to Beatrix from Putterskraal on December 8 reveals the extent of his alarm and exasperation:

'I am frightfully busy and worried. The whole of this country is seething with rebels, and as they are all mounted, and I have only a few mounted infantry on half-fed ponies, it is very difficult to cope with them.

'I have now three regiments of infantry, but have a long railway line to guard, and every culvert has a couple of armed men in it. Fancy what an anxiety this is — their safety, their food, their overworked condition. If I had my Division I could really strike somewhere . . .

'I am hoping to move on a bit tomorrow or the next day to recover some of the country given up prior to my arrival, as I think occupation of a position in advance of this may tend to awe the Dutch behind me.'

The key to the Eastern Cape was Stormberg Junction, a railway intersection some sixteen kilometres north of Molteno where the main line between Bloemfontein and East London met a branch line from Naauwpoort via Rosmead. Situated in a shallow basin surrounded by hills, it had only a month previously been in British hands before an ordered withdrawal had allowed the Boers to resume their occupation. It was at this garrison that Gatacre decided to aim his blow.

Not long after my arrival at Skemerfontein, I visited Stormberg Junction. It was a hot midsummer's morning with a cool wind flattening the grass on the plain and buffeting the few prickly-pear thickets and the trees around the settlement. Stopping at the station, I scanned the surrounds, noting immediately that they were little different from the way English journalist George Steevens had recorded them in 1899: 'The wind screams down from the naked hills onto the little junction station. A platform with dining-room and telegraph office, a few corrugated-iron sheds, the station-master's corrugated-iron bungalow — and there is nothing else of Stormberg but veldt and koppie, wind and sky . . .'

While I found that the station no longer had a dining-room or telegraph office, the station-master's bungalow was there, now occupied by a trader, its corrugated iron walls and roof still appearing sound at that high altitude where, so unlike Natal, nothing seems to corrode. There was also a drab waiting-room beside the Stormberg Junction signboard and several relatively new sheds flanking the railway between the station and the actual confluence of the lines several hundred metres to the north.

Crossing the tracks, I asked a black man, a labourer from a nearby farm and the sole occupant of the waiting-room, if he had heard of a battle there between the British and the Boers. 'No,' he replied, 'I am waiting for the train to Knysna which is coming tomorrow.' We spoke briefly of the coldness of the area in winter when, so I discovered later, the wind cuts like a razor through one's clothing and rakes up the dust in swirling spires and fierce eddies. I told him of my home near the sea in Natal where even in midwinter one seldom wears a jersey. He appeared momentarily incredulous, then laughed brightly and clapped his hands together in amazement. As we were talking a train appeared from the direction of Molteno, the sound of its diesel engines magnifying to a heavy throb as it sped past us without stopping and shrank into the distance towards Burgersdorp. 'Why don't you ask the baas about the battle?' ventured my companion, gesturing behind me. 'He will know.' Yes, I thought, and thanked him, returning to the district road and the store and house with its fence and fierce-dog warnings.

Mr Meiring, the trader, was thickset and surrounded by Dobermans. He had, he said, been trading there for twenty years. I asked, turning and pointing at Rooikop, the mountain which loomed above and beyond the station, whether the stone forts built half-way up it by the British were still standing.

'They're a bit broken but they're up there,' he replied, pointing at the dun-coloured grass and dark green besembos on the mountain.

It took me twenty minutes to clamber up the initial steep, stony slope. On reaching the crest, I located the remnants of two stone redoubts on the plateau and spent an hour clambering about them as the sun seared and the wind howled around me. Scattered middens of glass shards and tins lay among the tussocks and I combed through them for Lee-Metford doppies, finding only a small green ring which I took to be weathered brass and pocketed. (Here on my desk the blue base of a bottle also gleaned on that outing anchors the pages of several sheaf-copies of my Gatacre biography, preventing a swivelling fan from scattering them.)

It took little imagination to visualise the bored Tommies manning the pickets as they opened tins, slugged from bottles and scanned the distance for signs of the enemy. Far below was the junction with its railway line and the main Molteno-Burgersdorp road running beside it. Dwarfed by the immensity of the landscape, the tiny settlement seemed a paltry prize to fight over. In the distance to my left was the long mound of the Kissieberg behind which Gatacre had launched his abortive assault. Strategists conducting post mortems of the debacle say that to attack where I stood that morning on the right flank of Rooikop would have been infinitely better strategy. But post-wisdom is easy. In theory, Gatacre's plan of attack on the Boers encamped at Stormberg was impressive; only in practice did it fall disastrously short.

At the centre of Gatacre's strategy was the element of surprise. Instead of advancing ponderously from Putterskraal to Molteno and then, after an interval of preparation, continuing the remaining thirteen kilometres to Stormberg Junction, he decided to combine his advance and attack in a single rapid thrust. He would transport his infantry and guns by train to Molteno on the afternoon preceding the planned attack, march on Stormberg Junction by night and rush the Boer positions at dawn. Moving rapidly, and without dallying, he was sure that he'd catch the burghers unawares.

Militarists find little to fault this bold strategy but warn of the necessity for perfect execution. Even minor snags, they caution, would jeopardise everything. There should be no delays in the entrainment and there should be no danger of the troops losing their way during the night march. To prevent both from occurring, Gatacre had been particularly careful: he had delayed his advance from Putterskraal by a day to allow for the accumulation of sufficient railway trucks; he had ascertained that the moonlight would be strong on the evening of December 9; and he had planned to lead the night march along the railway line from Molteno to Stormberg Junction and thus exclude any chance of going astray.

However, ineptitude and misfortune dogged the operation from the start. A telegram to Major Springer and Captain De Montmorency (the latter of Omdurman fame) at Penhoek, ordering them to cover the right flank during the attack and to cut off the anticipated Boer retreat to Burgersdorp, was never sent by the clerk at Putterskraal station. With no timely attempt made to confirm its reception, the Penhoek detachment missed the defeat which their presence may have averted.

Also, the preliminary advance of thirty-five kilometres from Putterskraal to Molteno was delayed when a truckload of mules blocked the railway line. Consequently the journey took the entire day and although Gatacre had planned for a rendezvous in Molteno before sunset, his weary troops were still arriving as late as eight o'clock after waiting hours in the blazing sun. The town was abuzz with rumours as the two thousand-odd soldiers massed in the semi-darkness, some talking to the townsfolk and trading army biscuits and tins of bully beef for homebaked delicacies. Witnesses told of the weary men eyeing the conviviality in the Central Hotel enviously as they waited to begin their march.

Unknown to them, Gatacre had just completely altered his plan. Having arrived in Molteno early in the afternoon, he had spent several hours conferring with the local detachment of the Cape Police and had been informed — incorrectly, it turned out — that the Boers were entrenched behind barbed-wire entanglements at the very position which he planned to attack. Using this information, he decided to abandon his direct, frontal assault and instead to attack one of the supposedly undefended flanks. Wrongly, in the subsequent opinion of militarists, he didn't choose the right flank near Rooikop (where I searched the stone redoubts for doppies nearly a century later), but instead decided to advance along the Steynsberg road, cut across country and attack the left face of the Kissieberg.

Why didn't he choose the supposedly preferable right flank? We can only assume that he expected that Rooikop and its environs would be taken care of by the Penhoek detachment. Unknown to him as he and his weary troops began their final advance along the Steynsberg road shortly after nine o'clock, Springer, De Montmorency and their four hundred men, oblivious of the attack, were miles away at Penhoek preparing for bed.

Another query arising from the military coroners' autopsies of the defeat was why Gatacre decided to continue late on that Saturday evening. Surely he must have forseen problems with his exhausted troops and the prospect of navigating unchartered veld in the darkness. No longer did the British have a railway line to follow; everything depended on their guides, Inspector Neyland and Sergeant Morgan of the Cape Police, who professed an intimate knowledge of the neighbouring terrain. Gatacre and his troops were, in effect, some two thousand blind men following two supposedly sighted men through the night.

Despite the loss of surprise, the military coroners are emphatic that a prudent general would have delayed the attack until the following night, allowing his troops time to rest and first reconnoitring the new route in daylight. After all, the Boers were still expecting a frontal, not flanking, attack. But we mustn't forget the 'Backacher' syndrome — Gatacre's deification of fitness and his contempt of fatigue — and Koos Roussouw's allegation that he was set on exploiting the Sabbath. Both played their part.

To what extent were Gatacre's troops really exhausted that evening? Granted, they were predominantly unseasoned recruits new to the rigours of colonial service under a vicious sun, but they were also youthful and itching for a fight. Historical sources confirm their exhaustion although Beatrix Gatacre's whitewashing is singularly partial on this point: 'Indeed so eager were the men [she writes] that they set out at an unusually brisk pace.' That, we can be certain, is rubbish, as the troops' actions in the impending battle will confirm.

Something which compounded the troops' fatigue was a foolish order for them to march with fixed bayonets. This meant holding their rifles extended in front of them as they marched, a stance both awkward and exhausting.

Before long Gatacre was lost. After several hours marching, he and his column reached a railway crossing known to be three kilometres beyond the point where they had planned to branch off into the veld. He challenged his guides who denied going astray and explained that they had merely detoured to avoid a fence and a patch of uneven ground which would hamper the artillery. Uneasy, he called an hour's halt. Many of his men lay down and promptly fell asleep. This railway line which crossed the road was in fact a tributary leading from the Rosmead/Stormberg line to a nearby colliery. When, shortly after resuming their march, the soldiers crossed another line, Gatacre assumed it to be the Rosmead/Stormberg line when it was really the same colliery line which had looped around them. His confusion was now complete and for the remainder of the advance he was convinced that he was kilometres to the north of where he actually was.

Unknown to him, a section of his column was enacting a travesty of an advance nearby. On the departure of the infantry from Molteno, the artillery, support services and mounted troops were scheduled to follow at intervals. However, a body of men under a Colonel John Edge of the Royal Army Medical Corps and comprising the field hospital, bearer company and the maxim of the Irish Rifles, being oblivious of Gatacre's change of plan, had set out on the original route to the Junction. Along the road they encountered several journalists who, having failed to find Gatacre, were returning to Molteno to ask directions. Edge halted and awaited the journalists' return. Waking Colonel Wallscourt Waters, the officer left in charge of the village, the journalists were incorrectly assured that they were indeed on the correct route. That Waters, who had been present during Gatacre's meeting that afternoon with local members of the Cape Police, was himself in the dark, emphasises the extent of the confusion. Amazed, the journalists galloped back and met Edge who had in the meantime decided to return to Molteno. On being informed that he was in fact on the correct road, Edge wearily turned once again and continued northwards. At 2.30a.m. they met five policemen and two mule wagons, one of which carried the reserve ammunition of the Northumberland Fusiliers, who were also lost. Wisely, Edge decided to wait where he was until dawn. Shortly afterwards, two of Gatacre's staff officers who too were lost joined them. There they all waited while several kilometres to the north-west Gatacre and his column blundered blindly in the direction of the Kissieberg.

At about 3a.m. Gatacre's troops, still four abreast and with fixed bayonets, stumbled northwards into a dark basin and began to advance across it. Vaguely visible on their immediate right was a long flat mountain irregularly fringed with cliffs. Unknown to Gatacre, who was still completely disorientated, this mountain was the Kissieberg. He was, in other words, precisely where he wanted to be without knowing it.

The guides, aware of their whereabouts but thinking that the General was now merely intent on entering the Stormberg valley by road, never bothered to enlighten him. As the troops passed Van Zyl's farmhouse and advanced wearily across the donga and along the Kissieberg, unknown to them the Boers were encamped just over the brow. Most of the burghers were still asleep but a few were chatting and smoking pipes while their servants brewed coffee.

That each side was so close to the other neither knew at first, until something alerted the Boers. Historical sources differ about what ended the mutual ignorance. Some guess that the glint of a bayonet in the gathering dawn, or the chink of a shod hoof on a stone, gave the game away. Another says that it was the sound of Van Zyl shooting at the ravenous British stragglers as they slaughtered his pregnant ewes. Yet another says that a burgher wished to defecate and walked some distance from the camp to do so. As he squatted, he reputedly peered into the basin and detected the long column advancing through the gloom. Pulling up his trousers, he sprinted back over the brow, shouting: 'The khakis! The khakis! Here they come.'

Shots began to ring out. Gatacre, who had been walking beside his horse at the head of the column, ordered his leading battalion, the Irish Rifles, to take a hill to the north. However, only three companies responded. With bullets spattering around them, the remainder, including the Northumberland Fusiliers, attacked the Kissieberg. Some began to scale the less precipitous initial slope but on reaching the krantz that ringed most of the mountain, the majority gave up and, exhausted nearly beyond reason, found cover and promptly fell asleep. There, snug within a long shallow cave with its Bushman paintings, they huddled together like lambs on a winter night, their gentle snoring contrasting strangely with the gunfire around them.

Meanwhile, as Hennie Lotter asserted, the sound of Van Zyl's shooting at the rear of the column had increased the confusion. Were they being ambushed? That thought must have crossed Gatacre's mind as he tried to transform the chaos into a cohesive assault.

I first took Katie to visit the battlefield one cold morning in midwinter. Leaving the bakkie alongside the track that crosses the basin, we walked through a flock of cropping sheep, skirted the small cemetery, and eventually reached the long, shallow cave at the foot of the Kissieberg where the exhausted soldiers had sought refuge. There, beneath the overhang, with the icy wind sweeping down the slope and worrying the grass tussocks and besembos, we were suddenly and inexplicably overcome with randiness. Saying nothing, we embraced briefly before removing our jeans and coupling beside the faint outlines of the Bushman paintings. Clad only in jerseys and socks, the cold goose-fleshing our exposed haunches, we raced to a climax among the ant-lion traps and dried sheep droppings, our cries like those of the wounded soldiers.

Katie used that session like a crowbar, often prising open my research and scribblings with bawdy recollections of it. For me there remain two dominant images: the imprint of the cave floor on her buttocks, and her pinkness beside the drabness of the winter landscape.

The actions of the artillery both lost and saved the day. While those men of the Northumberland Fusiliers and Irish Rifles who had managed to find gaps in the Kissieberg krantz began their ascent towards the crest, the gunners wheeled to the left and crossed the valley. Reaching a suitable position from which to shell the heights, they unlimbered, positioned the guns and began their bombardment. At this point the sun appeared over the Kissieberg. Blinded by the blaze, the gunners aimed too low, raining shrapnel over the vanguard of their own infantry and wounding the aptly named Colonel Eager and six others.

While some sources claim that the attack had already faltered, the shelling accident triggered the rout. Having endured danger and exhaustion, even the stalwarts broke after the bombardment. Under heavy fire, the disheartened men fled down the hillside and across the plain.

Gatacre, desperate for a renewed assault, realised its impossibility. On the left, the three companies of the Irish Rifles were holding out but lacked the strength to attack without support. With the collapse of the right he had no alternative but to cut his losses and order a general retreat to Molteno.

Had the Boers' fire been more accurate, the fleeing British would have been decimated. Instead, as it turned out, there were remarkably few casualties, although historical sources abound with eyewitness accounts.

On descending from the Kissieberg and reaching the vacated battlefield, Jacobus Petrus Bosman, a young Boer schoolmaster, told of his finding a British soldier with both legs shattered sitting back against an anthill calmly smoking a cigarette. Bosman's response was hearteningly humane: 'Suddenly we were enemies no more, but friends, human beings in the fullest sense. Would I have been so calm and collected in such a maimed condition?'

While the Boers continued, moving through the dead and wounded, they were startled by the sound of a single shot. On investigating they found that a Tommy had ended the agony of his friend who had been shot through the kidneys by putting a bullet through his head.

Of the retreat under fire itself, a jingoistic tome published eighteen months after the battle provides the following rather graphic and melodramatic account by an unnamed soldier:

Many are hit severely, but continue to keep up, their comrades supporting them. There is one of the Northumberlands, with his hand shot clean away; another with his back broken by a splinter of shell. Another drags along for a few yards with his entrails hanging out. Then he gasps, 'It's no good! Goodbye!' and dies. The poor blacks of the transport service suffer just as heavily. Here one leaps into the air and drops in a heap. A bullet has broken his spine. There is another, trying to hop home, one foot nothing but a bleeding pulp. Pelted by that awful storm, the men stumble on. Here and there a subaltern or a sergeant collects a little force and forms a firing party; but the only men who are really of use are the artillery.

Fortunately for the British, the Boers were more interested in scouring the battlefield for loot than mopping up the stragglers. Only when a number of burghers assembled on high ground beyond the colliery line and began firing at the British rear, did they pose a real threat. This, however, was short-lived because the redoubtable Major Perceval hastily swung three of his field guns in their direction and silenced them. Thereafter the burghers merely followed — to quote from the *Times History* — like 'curs yapping after a man with a stick'.

During the course of the morning, the remnants of the column reached Molteno. The startled inhabitants, who had witnessed the ordered advance the previous evening, stared in disbelief as the vanquished troops stumbled back down the dusty street.

With casualties appearing light, Gatacre hoped to dismiss the defeat as merely an unsuccessful skirmish during a reconnaissance mission. It was only when he realised that a third of his force was missing that the full extent of the calamity became apparent. Devastated, he over-reacted and ordered a retreat to as far back as Queenstown before rallying slightly and settling on the nearer Sterkstroom. Arthur Conan Doyle records that Gatacre was seen sobbing in the Molteno railway station, bewailing the fate of his poor lost boys.

Incredibly, the six hundred and thirty-four officers and men, among them those who had sought refuge in the Kissieberg cave, hadn't been killed but left behind. Exhausted and disheartened, none of them had offered any resistance when the victorious Boers appeared, and all were taken prisoner.

No longer, Gatacre must have realised, could the defeat be underplayed. It was a disaster. He was responsible for the first major defeat of the war. His Stormberg shambles had started Black Week and with Magersfontein and Colenso would make world headlines. Things would never be the same again.

In all the fighting, in fact, only twenty-eight of Gatacre's force were killed and ten officers and fifty-one men wounded (among them Colonel Eager, who died later from his wounds), while the Boers lost only six men with twenty-seven wounded. Being god-fearing victors, theirs was the responsibility for burying the British dead. Digging shallow trenches in the stony ground, they bundled in the dead Tommies. Two days later, after the corpses had bloated, several belt buckles became visible in the soil, necessitating exhumation of the bodies, further excavation and reburial.

FIFTEEN

Poor old Gatacre; he really fucked it up. His reputation, meticulously built up over decades of zealous service, was dashed by a single gamble that failed. The following letter, written by him to Beatrix three days after the battle, encapsulates his feelings: 'The fault was mine, as I was responsible of course. I went rather against my better judgement in not resting the night at Molteno, but I was tempted by the shortness of the distance and the certainty of success. It was so near being a brilliant success.'

Of course, going against one's better judgement is always questionable, especially when one is a general in a perilous situation far from home. But what options did Gatacre have? Undermanned, overtaxed, with the enemy sweeping the countryside, he had to do something. And short of retreating, there wasn't much he could do except attack. As he confided in Beatrix before the battle, he needed to bloody the enemy's nose and bolster flagging confidence amidst widespread disaffection. That his blow would be inaccurate, or his opponent would jink, were chances he had to take. And doing nothing would have been contemptible, and suicidal.

Also, to have expected greater prudence from someone like Gatacre would have been nonsensical, *vide* the capture of the murderers near Quetta and the breaching of the Dervishes' zeriba at Atbara. That he executed the attack ineptly is true, but the Anglo-Boer War abounds with examples of ineptitude. His crime, quite simply, was that he failed and failure is inexcusable, especially when so much is expected of you as the following quote from a jingoistic newspaper early in the war reveals: 'This [the central column] was perhaps the most important expedition in the campaign, and, as the Boers have spent their strength upon the eastern and western frontiers, General Gatacre may be able to make a dash over the open country upon Bloemfontein, which, if it

does not stagger humanity, will at least astonish the world.'
Astonish the world! I can hear the general's hollow laughter.

Buller was understanding, supporting Gatacre's choice of tactics and commiserating with him over his bad luck, but he too was doomed, being only days away from his own nadir. Lord Roberts, Buller's successor, then commanding the British forces in Ireland, wouldn't be so accommodating, as Gatacre was soon to discover.

SIXTEEN

With the onset of winter came the iciness. For someone accustomed to subtropical torpor, it was exhilarating at first, but when the vice really tightened I retreated into the warmth of my research and observed the valley through the large window in my sitting-room. On windless days a hard clarity froze the landscape into starkness before the wind resumed, spuming the dust and gentling the demarcations into the likeness of a wash drawing. After a run of frosts so heavy that even the diesel froze in a tractor left out overnight and icicles dangled like ear-rings from the garden taps, came the snow, sifting softly downwards through the darkness and transforming the sheep into grubby huddles on the whiteness.

When lambing began, the pregnant ewes were moved to a camp beside the sheds and on several icy evenings Angus, Katie and I performed obstetrics by torchlight and carried to the scullery for cosseting those lambs rejected by their mothers. Usually the wind howled and buffeted the encircling poplars, tremoring their silver boles in the moonlight as we worked, our hands sticky with afterbirth.

Following parturition came thoughts of conception, the production line demanding constant attention. As one of a syndicate sharing a champion ram, Angus's turn came one freezing morning when Hennie Lotter arrived with the giant merino on the back of his bakkie. Wrapped in a sheepskin jacket and wearing an army bush-hat pulled low over his ears, Hennie greeted us cheerily and, as the ram was being off-loaded, lapsed almost immediately into a conversational overdrive, alternately on the open road or darting between subjects like a fugitive. Of our conversation I can remember very little, except his anecdote about the fate of farmer Van Zyl, zealous protector of pregnant ewes and potter of Gatacre's stragglers. Hennie's precise words, of course, are lost but like so much of this reminiscence, memory provides the skeleton which imagination fleshes out.

Backed by the spectacle of several labourers deferentially guiding the ram from the loading ramp into a shed, Hennie told of how soon after the battle one of Van Zyl's black labourers reported his shooting of several British soldiers to the authorities and how he was arrested and court-martialed. Despite his plea that he was merely defending his own property, he was sentenced to death. However, a timely general pardon by Lord Kitchener saved him from a firing squad in Burgersdorp and so great was his gratitude that he became something of an Anglophile. After the war, unlike most Afrikaners who were still deeply resentful, he opted for co-operation and became a Smuts supporter, establishing a verligte tradition maintained by subsequent generations of his family. It was not long, however, before he began to be plagued by guilt and he had a premonition that he would die on a specific date. As the day neared, his family gathered in solemn anticipation. When it passed without incident, he was given the sobriquet 'Doodgaan' and was encumbered by it for the remainder of a long life.

'You see, Jerry,' Hennie said on parting, 'God protected Van Zyl because what he did was right.'

'Yes,' I said, 'I must include that in my book,' meaning not so much the possibility of divine intervention but that someone as erudite as Hennie believed it to be possible.

Once the lambing was over, Katie returned to university and I resumed my celibate existence of researching and rambling. During those months of separation we phoned each other frequently and on two occasions I spent weekends with her in Grahamstown. After my somewhat ascetic life-style on the farm, those interludes among bohemian art students provided the fillip I needed to overcome my occasional crises of confidence. With their broad racial tolerance and enthusiasm for the future, the students were a useful reminder that those pockets of bigotry on the platteland had their counterpoints elsewhere.

During this period, my relationship with Katie increased steadily in intimacy but I have intentionally refrained from washing too much of our linen in public. Had our relationship ended on my return to Natal, I would have been more forth-coming but its continuation demands a certain reticence.

In early spring a team of Basotho shearers arrived and an annual ritual began. Bolstered by several of the Skemerfon-tein staff, they set to work immediately, plucking protesting animals from a penned flock and with great dexterity depriving them of their fleeces. From time to time I wandered down the hillside to the large shed and watched as each sheep was transformed from dirty rotundity to clean leanness, patterned with bloody nicks. For weeks the process continued: shorn ewes, hamels and rams scampering out into the sunlight as others were collared and contorted while their fleeces were peeled by the clippers. And then, as suddenly as they had arrived, the shearers moved on, leaving a silent shed piled high with bales of wool.

As the weather warmed so I began to extend my walks beyond the now familiar mountaintop to its furthermost slopes, finding barely accessible nooks and crannies among the rocks high above the Roussouw's little homestead. There, amid the stench of bat urine and dassie droppings, I found vague signs of human habitation: faded drawings, fire sites, smoke stains and doppies; all reminders of the grim games of hide-and-seek that have been played over the centuries in that mountain fastness. Musing on the participants — Bushmen pursued by Xhosas; Xhosas by Boers; Boers by British — I detected a pattern which seemed heavy with foreboding.

After snooping among the rocks, I sometimes paid the Roussouws a visit, descending to their cottage with its scuffing chickens and Heath Robinsonesque clothesline strung haphazardly between several disused implements and an assortment of stunted fruit trees. Often Naas was alone, Koos and Oom Piet being away in Toomnek or Fluis-tervlakte or attending to some agricultural matter, and we would sit on the stoep and talk and drink tea. Once we had emptied the pot of rooibos and a portly maid had removed the tray, Naas would invariably invite me to see his collection of firearms or his guinea-fowls which he kept in an enclosure in the yard. Leading me through the voorkamer to a gun safe, he would unlock it with difficulty and then remove a selection of rifles and shotguns, enthusing about each as he explained its workings.

Placing them side by side on the dining-room table in a position that suggested organ pipes, Naas would indicate each and croon about its peculiarities. And time and again I would feign fascination when I was really only intrigued by the abnormality of his engrossment.

During my last visit he disappeared into the house after we had drunk our customary pot of rooibos on the stoep and returned with a Mauser in one hand and an R1 in the other. 'This,' he announced in his peculiar bray, indicating the Mauser, 'is the gun we used to shoot the British. And this,' brandishing the R1, 'is the one that we are using to shoot the kaffirs. These are our best friends.' He laughed heartily and I reciprocated, mirthlessly, struck once again by how he had completely disregarded my cultural origins and like Anna Strydom had never doubted that I too hated blacks.

Shadowed by two boerbuls, he then led me to a wire enclosure among several peach and apple trees. Opening a gate, he stepped inside and dropped to his haunches, uttering a sound like that of a suckling calf. Promptly, some twenty guinea-fowls burst from the long grass and jostled for the mealies in his outstretched hand. Delighted by their enthusiasm, he guffawed, saliva dripping from his chin, and caressed several birds as they pecked at his palm. As I watched him through the veil of wire, it was hard not to like him, racism and all.

Later, leaving the enclosure, he showed me the intricate web of trip-wires that he had rigged along its perimeter to protect his birds from thieves. The dogs, he said, slept inside at night, so if he heard any sound outside, he shot first and checked later. If he didn't take these precautions, everything would be stolen.

As I wandered home over the mountain that afternoon, I found myself pondering on Naas's preoccupation with protection. Typically of whites in this country, he was haunted by dispossession. Both his life-style and his possessions, he felt, were coveted by the already dispossessed and somehow he *had* to protect them.

SEVENTEEN

Scarcely two and a half months after the Stormberg debacle, fate dealt Gatacre another crippling blow: Captain Jim de Montmorency, a legendary figure and by all accounts his most gifted young officer, was killed in action. Morale plummeted. Gatacre was stunned; it was as if he had been floored by his defeat and now fate was putting in the boot.

Jim de Montmorency or, more formally, the Honourable Raymond Hannay Lodge Joseph de Montmorency, was shot dead during a skirmish on the farm Weltevreden several miles north-east of Molteno on February 23, 1900. The eldest son of a viscount and major general, he had eighteen months previously, as a lieutenant in the 21st Lancers, braved an avalanche of frenzied Dervishes to save a fallen comrade. Although the fellow officer had already died, De Montmorency and his accomplice, one Sergeant Byrne, extricated the body, an act for which both received the Victoria Cross. To this decoration De Montmorency added the British medal and the Khedive's medal and clasp. Promoted to captain in 1899, and sent out to South Africa on special service, he assembled a band of seventy-odd daredevils which operated with great effect in the Stormberg and Dordrecht districts. Being mounted and therefore manoeuvrable, Montmorency's Scouts confronted the Boers on equal terms and, unlike the ponderous British divisions, were often victorious.

Soon after my arrival at Skemerfontein, I expressed a desire to see where De Montmorency was killed. Phoning the owner of the farm on my behalf, Angus organised the visit and I set out early one afternoon, travelling first to Molteno and then northwards along a district road flanking a railway line; in fact following the same route Gatacre had intended to take before changing his mind that fateful afternoon. Several kilometres from Molteno the road bore right, leaving the railway line and scything through the grasslands, and shortly thereafter I saw the farm's signpost.

Turning up the bumpy track, I arrived at a small yard behind a nondescript white bungalow. Between the few outbuildings and the back verandah was parked a bakkie and beside it, seated on a wooden box, was a black girl washing clothes in an oval galvanised iron tub. She was fat and slovenly in appearance, and, seemingly oblivious of my presence, continued pummelling a pair of trousers as the dust stirred by my arrival billowed around her.

'Afternoon,' I said in Afrikaans, as a Natalian being only conversant in Zulu and not in the Xhosa spoken by blacks in the Stormberg. 'Can I speak to the baas?'

'The baas, he's inside,' she mumbled, rousing herself and scuffing slowly towards the verandah.

I waited near the other bakkie, noticing an army rifle in the passenger footwell, its flash-hider protruding from the open window, and a full magazine on the seat beside it. Stealing both would be so easy, I remember thinking. Such lax security would infuriate the authorities.

Presently a large young man wearing black rugby shorts and a T-shirt distended by his paunch appeared and greeted me cheerily in Afrikaans. 'You're the chap Mr Murray phoned about.'

'Yes,' I smiled and nodded.

'The stone is there on the hill. You can drive up to a camp, and then you must walk. I'll get my boss boy to show you.' He turned to the girl. 'Go get Willem,' he instructed, his tone that blend of authority and familiarity which I often encountered in speech between similar people in similar locations. The girl left her washing and ambled off with suds dripping from her fingers.

I indicated his rifle and we spoke briefly about national service. He'd been in the infantry and had done his basic training at Ladysmith.

'Jussus, but that's a hot place,' he exclaimed, his full lips mobile beneath his sparse moustache.

He was now a member of the local commando and had that morning returned from a stint of township duty. Agitators had apparently been at work in the Toomnek township and the commando had been sent in to contain the sporadic violence. Nothing serious, he assured me, apparently feeling that I needed reassurance. 'But if there's more shit, don't worry, the men are ready.' He hesitated, as if about to continue, but then an elderly black man in a blue overall appeared.

'Willem,' said the youth, 'take the baas to that soldier's stone.'

'Yes baas,' replied the headman, crossing to a gate between two outbuildings and opening it.

'Would it be all right if I took him with me?' I asked.

'Willem? Yes, sure,' he exclaimed, 'don't worry, he's a good kaffir.'

'Thanks,' I said, sardonically, getting into my bakkie and driving through the gate Willem had opened. Willem then climbed in beside me and we drove slowly up the hillside, crossing a camp whose cropped grass crunched beneath the bakkie's tyres, until we reached a barbed-wire fence.

'We must now walk,' he said in Afrikaans, parting the strands for me and then leading the way across rock-strewn grassland and between clumps of besembos towards the koppie's summit.

After about ten minutes we reached a cairn of dun stones crowned by a heart-shaped granite plaque on which was inscribed with moving simplicity the following few words:

HERE THE BRAVE
MONTMORENCY
FELL
23rd FEB
1900

The memorial, so Angus had told me, had been erected some thirty years after Montmorency's death by his elderly sister who had come out from England to visit the place where he had been killed, and his grave in Molteno.

Standing there, with Willem silent beside me, I scanned the surrounding veld. Several miles to the north-west were

113

both the Kissieberg and Rooikop, their profiles sharpened by the sinking sun. From that vantage point the theatre encompassing Gatacre's fall and Montmorency's death seemed so small beside the endlessness of the plains and koppies. Had I had the necessary elevation, I could have seen it all: the coveted junction with its two blockhouses; Van Zyl's house; the remains of the British redoubts on Rooikop from which I had pilfered the brass ring, glass shards and rusted tins; the site of Gatacre's rout and the route of his retreat. So many destinies, it seemed, were met within that vicinity, whipped as it always is by a wind of peculiar irritability.

The manner of Montmorency's death has been well recorded. Reports have it that a chastened Gatacre had advanced cautiously from Sterkstroom on Friday, February 23, reoccupying Molteno and reconnoitring the Boer positions at Stormberg, his left flank covered by the Cape Police and his right by Montmorency and his Scouts. Assuming the reconnaissance to be the vanguard of a major attack, the Boers had descended in force from Rooikop and galloped towards the koppie where I was then standing. On hearing that the Boers were rushing it from the north, Montmorency and several of his Scouts did likewise from the south. However, Montmorency and his men were hampered by the steepness of the southern slope and were forced to dismount while the Boers sped uninterruptedly towards the summit from the north, arriving first by a matter of seconds. A fierce skirmish ensued at a range of forty yards, during which Montmorency and three of his scouts were shot dead. Shot through the stomach, pitching forward into the grass, Montmorency fired at the Boers for several minutes before he died.

Six more Scouts died in the skirmish which ended with a British withdrawal to Molteno during the sudden thunderstorm. Throughout that night Montmorency's corpse and those of his comrades lay sodden on the koppie as the driving rain streamed from the snub leaves of the besembos and ran in rivulets through the mosaic of rocks and boulders.

In Molteno, Sergeant Byrne, Montmorency's soldier-servant with whom he had won the VC at Omdurman, was distraught, spending the night weeping beside his master's Arab charger, and had to be restrained the following morning from galloping out alone to retrieve the body of his master. Later a party led by two chaplains bearing a white flag sought permission to recover the bodies. This the Boers granted, but when the party reached the koppie it was incensed to find that the corpses had been stripped of their clothing, and that a Boer was wearing Montmorency's slouch hat with its skull-and-crossbones insignia and black ostrich feather plume. To the Tommies, such effrontery was sacrilege, an act tantamount to the defilement of an icon in the presence of zealots, but in their helplessness they could do nothing except sullenly recover their fallen comrades.

That Sunday the dead were buried in the Molteno cemetery and a grieving Gatacre attended the service, standing erect beside the row of graves as a regimental band played mournfully. Such was the blow to his confidence that this tragedy, added to his Stormberg reversal, seemed temporarily to have stunned him. Even when Kitchener ordered an advance on Stormberg Junction, Gatacre was markedly hesitant, being without Montmorency's support, until other troops cleared his flanks. However, another factor played its part: with the Boers' major defeat at Paardeberg, a general retreat of their forces was ordered, allowing the British to take the coveted junction on March 5, 1900 without firing a shot.

And so Gatacre at last achieved his objective, if only by default. The victor was a very different man from that who had advanced eagerly, although apprehensively, only four months previously. He appeared taciturn and withdrawn, as if his succession of reverses had soused much of the fire that usually burned so noticeably within his wiry frame.

On returning to the bakkie, I thanked Willem and gave him a tip before descending to the farmhouse. The slovenly maid, still washing outside, left her suds and escorted me into the sitting-room where the youth was lying back in an armchair drinking beer and watching television. Declining an offer of a drink, I thanked him and left, but, seemingly wanting to talk, he followed me outside, beer can in hand.

'You must come back sometime,' he said. 'There is a British fort right up at the top of the farm. We must ride there on horses. No one goes there and the ground is still full of doppies.'

'Yes, thank you,' I replied, 'I would like to see it very much.'

On my way home through Molteno, I visited the cemetery, finding the graves in the twilight, a row of pale crosses beneath a large pine. The tallest memorial, topped by a Celtic cross, listed those killed: Capt R.H. de Montmorency V.C., Lieut. Col. Hoskier — Middlesex Volunteer Artillery (attached), Corporals A.R. Rudd and J. Weatherley, and Scouts F.S. Collett, L.A. Maasdorp and H. Vice, the penultimate name revealing the colonial character of the unit.

It was dark when I left the cemetery and set off towards Skemerfontein, my head filled with thoughts of the futility of war and memories of friends killed in action in Rhodesia, Angola and South West Africa. Less than an hour later I reached Toomnek, its cluster of lights dulled by a pall of smoke which had drifted across from the black township. Stopping at a cafe to buy a loaf of bread, I found the three Roussouws inside. Looking characteristically dishevelled, they were seated around one of the formica-topped tables provided for customers, watching football on a television set mounted among shelves of tinned food. From time to time the Portuguese proprietor erupted, jabbering excitedly at some instance of good play or a foul, and engaged the Roussouws in an animated discussion in a quaint, heavily-accented amalgam of English and Afrikaans. I greeted them all, requested the bread, and waited while the proprietor, transfixed by some infringement on the screen, fumbled with the loaf and like a Braille reader calculated my change in the open tray of his till.

While I waited, Naas rose from his chair and buttonholed me, braying 'How's it going with the general?'

'Well, thank you Naas,' I replied. 'Every day he becomes more real.'

'That's good Jerry. To hear that makes me very pleased.' He clapped me gently on the back and shuffled back to his father and brother.

Climbing into the bakkie, I drove slowly down the main street, passing the Masonic lodge and the primary school, and then accelerated onto the open road. Being hungry, I broke off chunks from the fresh loaf and ate them as I sped through the darkness.

EIGHTEEN

My last drinking session at the Royal Hotel was much like all the others and provided no inkling of what was to occur later that evening. Being a Thursday, only the true regulars were there, and none of the recreational drinkers who limited themselves to weekends. As the moribund discothéque then seemed to stir only on Saturdays, its throbbing music was once again absent, allowing the boxing videos to roar and clap unhindered.

Hennie Lotter, as much a feature of the bar as the dartboard and girlie calendar, was on good form, brimming over about everything, his erudition and repartee as sharp as ever. Encircling him, like fledglings around a food-proffering parent, was the usual selection of weathered farmers and begrimed artisans, all eager for his offerings.

Inevitably, as the usual concession to my presence, Gatacre was mentioned briefly towards the end of the evening. As a reluctant conscript bemoaning the frequency of army call-ups, Hennie chided the general for being so idiotic as to volunteer for a lifetime's military service. Conceding that Gatacre was only the third of four sons, Lotter still found it inconceivable that a gentleman who had a whole empire to choose from would consign himself to an existence of saluting and being saluted, with the added disincentive of a good chance of being killed. Surely, he ventured with the passion of fading sobriety, life as a planter in India, Malaya or some such far-flung corner was infinitely preferable. And some of the Eastern girls were so beautiful. And they would make such good companions after a hot evening's drinking on the verandah. And yet instead he chose the Stormberg and Reddersburg and had his troops either shot to pieces or captured by the enemy.

'Tell me, Jerry,' he intoned, his drinking arm unsteady and his beer slopping on the counter, 'what's better? Fucking under a mosquito net on your plantation in India or crying like a hyena in the Molteno railway station? Now don't tell me that Gatacre wasn't bloody stupid.'

'But,' I countered, 'you mustn't forget that Gatacre had a brilliant career before Stormberg and Reddersburg. Only right at the end did he cock things up.'

'Maybe, but he still failed.'

'Look,' I said, asking the barman for a pen and drawing two tiny black dots in the centre of the underside of a coaster. 'What can you see here?'

'Two dots,' he replied.

'No, no,' I exclaimed, delighted at his response. 'What you see is a big white expanse with two tiny dots in the centre.'

'And so?' ventured a farmer.

'Take the whole circle of cardboard to represent Gatacre's career and the two dots to mean Stormberg and Reddersburg. There's a hell of a lot of white that you're not seeing.'

'Ja, okay,' said Hennie, 'but there's still only really the dots.'

'Exactly,' I said, pedantically, 'that's the problem. People never see the whole picture.'

There was a pause before Hennie spoke again. As if to disperse the seriousness that had descended, his tone was buoyant: 'Ja, Jerry, but who really cares anyway?'

'Probably nobody,' I laughed, and the didactic interlude passed.

At closing time everyone congregated on the pavement for a last round of inanities before setting off homewards. Half-inebriated, and with Katie back in Grahamstown, I confess that I would have sought solace from Martie had she still been in the village. But, with no other option, I set off for Skemerfontein, driving slowly between the widely spaced street-lights, slicing the zones of glare and half shadow until everything became darkness and only the headlights probed a tunnel.

It being late winter, the night was cold and the rush of my bakkie's heater was a warm sound that accompanied me along the harsh, all-weather surface of the district road, its peacefulness interrupted only by the clatter of stones flung up into the mudguards by the wheels. At the summit of Boesmansnek a hare appeared, its white tail bobbing as it jinked in the glare of the headlights before veering off into the night. As the road fell away and began to spiral lazily towards Skemerfontein, I scanned the plain for the homestead's lights but saw nothing in the blackness, it being clearly too late and everyone long asleep.

And then I saw it. I was nearing the merino sign and had just dipped into the sloot where Naas had seen Gatacre amidst the milling sheep. Assuming the movement to be merely another hare, or a meerkat, I was only vaguely attentive until the headlights, rising out of the sloot, caught the man broadsides and held him motionless for a split-second, like an athlete frozen in a single frame of film. It was, I realised instantly, Elias Mbuyembu, the fugitive activist most wanted by the authorities, the man whose mug shot had entered countless homes country-wide over the previous few months. No sooner had our gazes met than he was gone, darting down the sloot as the headlights arced past him and illuminated the signpost several hundred metres ahead.

Momentarily I decelerated, perhaps with the unconscious intention of attempting a heroic capture, but then accelerated again. Now icy sober, my mind was in turmoil, some thoughts calling for police intervention and others for me to concede that what I had seen was merely a chimera conjured by alcohol. As I turned in the gate and drove slowly up the driveway, so the bombardment continued, wildly disparate thoughts rushing in at me like flotsam into a vortex. A strong lobby reiterated that the police must be called and the reward accepted or given to charity. Another attempted to give Mbuyembu's perspective; that of an educated man driven to rebel against injustice. Seeking no more than basic human rights, he was, said that part of me, as much a victim as his own victims. That three people had died because of his actions was an extremely regrettable by-product of his courageous idealism. Of course, as a white, this attitude would be difficult for me to understand. Cocooned by my privilege, I couldn't hope to grasp the extent of a black person's hurt and frustration in such an iniquitous system as ours. I would first have to suspend my inherent prejudices and try to understand what life is like on the other side of the racial divide. Only then would I appreciate Mbuyembu's true heroism and realise that his culpability in causing three deaths was in fact far less than that of millions of whites who bolstered a system that denied countless blacks their birthright.

Instead of stopping at the main house and waking the Murrays, I drove on between the sheds and up the mountainside to my cottage, persuading myself that I needed time to decide. I could even delay phoning until the following morning, explaining that I only realised it was Elias Mbuyembu after I saw his photograph in a back issue of the *Daily Herald* during breakfast. Not having a television of my own, I could easily deny knowing what he looked like. While both the Murrays and the Thorntons knew that I had seen Mbuyembu's face on television, that occasion was several months previously and I could plead forgetfulness. By delaying reporting him for eight or so hours, I would at least be giving him a sporting chance. Like a hunter using a shotgun rather than a rifle with telescopic sights, I was stacking only some of the odds in my favour. I could, therefore, be both law-abiding and do my bit for the struggle. Like a true liberal I could be as nice as possible to everyone.

I made a mug of coffee and collapsed into a deep armchair in the sitting-room. As I munched biscuits and sipped the coffee, I could see the telephone in the gaslight, looking as squat as a frog among my books on the oak table. As I sat there, transfixed by it, that part of me that advocated immediate action began to implore me to pick up the receiver, reassuring me with my right to anonymity. All the police needed was a tip-off. They could then take a dog (perhaps the same Doberman bitch which had nosed unsuccessfully for the desecrator) to the sloot and it would all be over in a couple of hours. I could then go to sleep knowing that the deaths of the elderly woman and the two teenage girls would be avenged. That, at least, they deserved, being innocent victims. Politics aside, it was merely a matter of bringing a murderer to book. If only to stop him killing others, Mbuyembu had to be caught, at all costs.

In spite of the fervour of my deductions, I did nothing that night. Resolving to report him first thing in the morning, I went to bed and slept remarkably soundly, waking at dawn to the reassuring sounds of the doves, the windmill, and Hester stoking the fire outside. Mulling over my resolution as I washed and shaved, I found myself making excuses for doing nothing. Mbuyembu, I told that diminishing part of me which still demanded action, would now be long gone, fearing recognition and wanting to put as much distance as possible between himself and the sloot. As it would be futile reporting him, seeing that he was probably already in Lesotho, I decided at breakfast to leave things as they were, willing myself to accept that I hadn't seen the fugitive but had merely thought that I had after an evening's drinking. Consequently, rather than inconvenience the police with a false lead, I wouldn't tell them anything.

As if in penance for my decision, I worked particularly hard that morning, transposing myself with Gatacre, stumbling about in the darkness west of the Kissieberg and dragging my troops through what was left of the night towards a dawn assault. By lunch I was saturated with history and decided to spend the afternoon walking on the mountain. Taking the path through the pines behind my cottage, and passing the cave with its paintings, I scrambled up the defile and reached the plateau with its vast view across the homestead, fields and expanse of grassland mole-hilled with koppies.

As I set off over the grass, my walking-stick swinging rhythmically, I found my thoughts returning to Elias Mbuyembu. Troubled by my decision to protect a murderer, I pondered the question of his culpability. Was he, I wondered, really responsible for the three deaths as stated on television? Or was it merely an allegation made by that state service to make him appear reprehensible? While virtually all blacks, most Indians and coloureds, and a growing number of whites wouldn't report a political activist to the authorities, they would assist in the arrest of a murderer. Perhaps that was the state's ploy in distorting a tenuous allegation into a fact and labelling him with the deaths. This possibility bolstered my decision and helped assuage my guilt. My response, I then told myself, had been the right one. I had rejected the past in favour of the future.

So absorbed was I with this conundrum that I reached the end of the mountain sooner than expected and stood for several minutes at the end of a spur which loomed over the upper reaches of the Skemerfontein valley where it converged with the Roussouws' gully. Far below the modest settlement was visible, and I looked for signs of life among the two simple buildings and an adjoining kraal, all encircled by small mealie fields. A cow was tethered to the base of the windmill near the rocky outcrop where I had first seen the three men stalking the rinkhals, and what appeared to be several chickens were eddying about among an assortment of implements and tractor remnants beyond the cottage. The back door was open and I toyed briefly with the idea of inviting myself to tea before deciding against it and heading homewards along the lip of the escarpment.

As I neared the water trough and windmill where the Doberman bitch had lost the desecrator's scent, I flushed a grey rhebuck and watched as it leapt rockingly though the grass with its tail curled up over its rump, before dissolving into a montage of rocks and ground cover in the distance. Choosing a circuitous route home, I traced a sheep track down the mountainside, meandering through scrub and boulders, and dipping from terrace to terrace towards the cemetery and the Murrays' homestead.

While I was walking, and staring abstractedly across the cultivated land in the valley, I noticed something bobbing several hundred metres to my left. Stopping, and shielding my eyes from the glare, I distinguished a portly black woman lumbering hurriedly along a farm track through the rye grass, her dress and apron flapping and her large breasts bouncing like helium balloons about to break their tethers.

Thinking no more about it, I continued to the cemetery, pausing at its stone wall to contemplate the as yet unrepaired memorial when the woman burst noisily from the poplars and yelled — 'The baas Naas, he's dead. He's stabbed with a knife in the kitchen. Where's the big baas? We must call him' — and, wheezing dramatically, blundered past me in the direction of the house. Jolted from my reverie, I sprinted to the sheds, crossed the yard and bounded through the front door shouting for Angus.

He appeared almost immediately from his study and I barked, 'Naas Roussow's been killed. Some woman's just told me. She's near the kitchen.'

'Good God,' he exclaimed, striding down the passage and speaking rapidly to the woman in Xhosa. Presently, turning to me, he said 'Let's get the police,' before grinding the telephone handle and asking in Afrikaans for the station commander. After a brief exchange, he grabbed a bunch of keys from the hall table and, gesticulating at the woman and me, strode out to the bakkie in the garage.

'We'll meet them there,' he said as we accelerated down the drive. 'Koos and the old man are away in Bloemfontein. Naas was alone in the house. Let's hope the poor fellow isn't really dead and we can do something for him.'

We drummed over the cattle grid beside the merino sign and gunned along the district road towards Fluistervlakte before bearing right behind the mountain and descending a bumpy track to the Roussouws' homestead. Throughout the journey Angus said only one sentence — 'I wonder who had a go at the poor fellow' — to which my response was merely an endorsement. Remarkably, it was only during the ensuing silence that I realised to my horror what had actually happened: in a rage, or mad funk, or crazed with hunger, Elias Mbuyembu had murdered Naas Roussouw. Nausea welled within me but I bottled it up in my determination to keep my secret. So long a benign bystander in the armed struggle, I had in only hours been tugged into the very centre of the melee. Never again, I knew then, could I remain detached; I had blood on my hands and although only I knew, its stain was indelible.

As Angus parked the bakkie, the maid flung open the door and we followed her hurriedly to the kitchen. There, seated on the floor, with his torso propped by the leg of a table and the corner of a coal stove, was Naas, his eyes open and his chin smeared with saliva and blood. Beside him lay an encrusted bread knife which was clearly the murder weapon. Stepping between the pools of congealed blood which linked much of Naas's immediate surrounds to the extensive wounds in his throat and neck, Angus felt his pulse and announced the obvious. With the urgency over, we moved outside as the police arrived in two bakkies, one of which had behind its cab a wire cage containing the Doberman bitch.

While the blue-uniformed figures made for the cottage, greeting us as they passed, I suddenly felt terrified that my guilt was patently obvious. Surely, I told myself, such trained eyes can detect tell-tale signs in my attempts at nonchalance. Surely they knew already that I was implicated but were merely feigning ignorance in the knowledge that I would soon let my cover slip.

The police made a brisk yet thorough inspection, their faces impassive as they stepped over Naas and combed the interior for clues. The white members, I remember thinking, had that air of grim tenacity that overcomes whites when one of their kind has fallen victim to what appears to be black violence. Their manner, although formal, seemed to urge a solidarity among all whites in the face of a common enemy. In other words, that afternoon beside Naas's corpse the police probably felt more kinship with me than they ever have, before or since. Such is the scope of irony.

Angus spoke briefly to the commander as one of the men took fingerprints and the dog handler primed the bitch, lifting the breadknife gingerly, a forefinger at each end, and holding it beneath her snout. We then left for Toomnek police station to make statements, and throughout the journey, during which Angus said nothing, I wrestled with my guilt. Perhaps Mbuyembu really had killed those three people in East London. Perhaps he really was nothing better than a common criminal operating under the guise of liberator.

Alternatively, knowing now that the police found no incriminating fingerprints of Mbuyembu's, either on the breadknife or anywhere else in the house, how can I be certain that he was in fact Naas Roussouw's killer? While I had seen him the previous evening, there was nothing to prove that he had killed Naas. Perhaps he had merely fled after my sighting, crossing farms by night and obtaining food from compliant labourers who have kept their secret. Perhaps he really is now in Maseru or Lusaka, embroiled in the struggle from outside, waiting with other exiles to return in triumph. As Angus and I neared Toomnek late that afternoon, dust billowing behind us, I was being torn by my two adversaries, that part of me which had advocated reporting him remaining convinced of his guilt, while the other voice, the one which I had heeded, laid snares of doubt in an attempt to ease my conscience.

We were still at the station when the commander returned from the Roussouws, having taken the corpse to the mortuary and left a constable to guard the house while the remaining policemen tagged behind the Doberman and her handler as she nosed across the veld. Relatives had also been informed and were en route to the farm with the dominee from Fluistervlakte to await Koos and Oom Piet's arrival.

As we left the charge office, I saw in an adjoining room the brawny sergeant who had arrived first at Skemerfontein after we had reported the desecration of the graves. Although he had soon returned to Toomnek to summon the dog squad, I had always associated him with the investigation. Seeing him there, rocking on his chair beneath the orange, white and blue tricolour, I felt a sudden urge to demand an explanation for the lack of progress but restrained myself, the defilement of two old memorials seeming so trifling beside a murder.

On our return to Skemerfontein, Angus invited me to supper and I agreed with alacrity, relieved that the solitude of my cottage would be postponed for several hours. As we sat around the fire in the sitting-room, eating off trays on our laps, the three of us reminisced about Naas and pondered the identity of his murderer. At times I felt that my guilt was obvious, especially after several beers, but I realised later that I was merely reading suspicion into Angus and Mary's demeanour when it certainly didn't exist. There was about

Naas, we all agreed, a feyness and simplicity that was endearingly anachronistic. Only his racism was disturbing, although Angus ventured that it was more innate than conscious.

'There was an innocence about Naas,' he said quietly as the fire snickered and wheezed. 'His racism was almost instinctual, like most people's hatred of snakes. It was more a fear than anything else, although I don't think he would have realised it.'

Safety was another topic discussed that night. The murder of a white in an isolated rural area called for greater security. As long as the killer was at large, no one could afford to take chances. Consequently, when I left, Angus insisted that I take with me one of his revolvers.

'We have another and two shotguns,' he said when I remonstrated. 'You owe it to Gatacre to look after yourself.'

NINETEEN

During the ensuing weeks my relationship with myself vacillated between two completely contrary stances: pride at my decision not to report Mbuyembu, and horror that I had been an accessory to a murder. Unable to reconcile the incidents, I had soon, with all the ingenuity of someone needing a panacea, separated them, applauding my emancipation from racial conditioning on the one hand, and sorrowing at the death of a friend on the other. Naas Roussouw's death, I conceded, did occur after my sighting of Mbuyembu, but the inability of the police to identify or apprehend the murderer left the possibility that he wasn't responsible. Taking my acquittal further, I counter-attacked, accusing myself of prejudice in linking a black fugitive with the murder of a white farmer. It was only racial indoctrination, I told myself, that made me assume that a white killed in such circumstances must have been the victim of a black and that Mbuyembu, being a fugitive from a white system, was bound to be the killer. So successful was my gerrymandering with the boundaries of blameworthiness that I soon became a fully-fledged member of the struggle who happened, quite fortuitously, to be also someone grieving the death of a friend.

My sighting of Mbuyembu, Naas's murder, and the subsequent exoneration of my guilt, all marked the beginning of the end of my stay at Skemerfontein. Overcome with listlessness, I did progressively less historical research and busied myself with reading novels and walking, merely whiling away the days until my lease expired. On those occasions when my absolution seemed inadequate and I felt particularly down, I phoned Katie at her digs in Grahamstown, telling her only of my loneliness and devotedness and not of the other impetus behind my call. And on each occasion her reciprocation of my affection and her assurances that she would spend the Christmas holidays with me in Natal buoyed my flagging resolve and ordered me back to Gatacre whose dismissal and public disgrace made my private agony seem less unendurable.

These bouts of comparing myself with the general proved extremely productive, impressing on me the need for stoicism, a quality which he had in abundance. Like Gatacre's, I told myself repeatedly, my intentions had always been honourable. Both of us were merely pawns in an unjust game, and that fate had chosen to conspire against us was a tactic we couldn't counter, but only attempt to endure. However, I knew that my action, unlike Gatacre's, had been victorious. While I too had suffered casualties, by vicariously assisting Mbuyembu I had crossed the fabled Rubicon, casting off from the past and drifting anxiously towards the future. Being driven to take that leap of faith in dramatic circumstances, my transition had been comparatively easy. Crossing quietly and deliberately through inner resolve, as most white South Africans would have to do, required far greater courage.

So devious were my machinations then that only now do I have the necessary distance to attempt to unravel them. Ingeniously, I hadn't merely ousted my guilt but transformed myself by default into something of a hero. Like a soldier frozen with fear who had been unable to flee a battlefield with his comrades after an unsuccessful engagement, but had miraculously survived, I appeared courageous. Had I been one of the farmers in the district I would most likely have made a citizen's arrest or at least phoned the police immediately. Mbuyembu would soon have been behind bars, on death row probably, and I would have received the reward and been the hero of a segment of the community. But by hesitating, initially through timidity rather than any other loftier reason, I had found myself in a predicament from which crossing the Rubicon seemed the easiest escape route. And now, having made good my getaway, I had Mbuyembu to thank for prompting it. That Naas, and possibly three others, had been killed in the process was its only flaw.

As the date of my departure neared, I felt a growing need to pay a last visit to the Stormberg battlefield. With December 10, the anniversary of the battle, falling during my last week of occupation, I chose it for my visit in the hope that with the sun in the same alignment the British assault could be as realistically imagined as possible. Such a crystallisation of that day's happenings, I told myself earnestly, would greatly assist my construction of the biography amidst the humidity and luxuriance of the Natal coast over the following year. Hushed by the tumbling rush of the surf, and with that last visit still clear in my mind, I would be able to look back and see with crystal clarity the exhausted khakis as they clambered between the rocks while the Mausers crackled like lightning along the spine of the mountain.

Setting out in the early hours, I took the usual route via Toomnek and Molteno, passing the Van Zyl homestead and entering the basin as the beginnings of dawn flushed the brow of the Kissieberg. Stopping beside the now familiar barbed-wire fence beyond which scatterings of sheep shuffled and cropped in the twilight, I boiled a mug of water on a gas cooker and sat back in a deckchair, waiting for the sun.

As I waited, as excited as a child at the cinema, drinking tea and munching shortbread, I let the reel of the battle run yet again in my mind, seeing a column of troops, four-abreast and with bayonets fixed, trudging through the mist. At its head, leading his horse by the reins, was Gatacre, a David Niven figure, only smaller and harder. Behind came the artillery, moving quietly, the wheels of the gun carriages wrapped in cowhide and only the harnesses jingling softly. Suddenly, rifle fire exploded from the heights to the right. Like a puff-adder blasted by shotgun pellets, the column segmented, each piece writhing, the Royal Irish Rifles running for the koppies to the front, the Northumberland Fusiliers rushing the mountain itself, and the artillery wheeling left-wards and galloping across the basin in search of a good position from which to begin shelling. Subalterns, young public school stereotypes, barked orders. Then the sun appeared over the brow, its rays almost horizontal. The Irish Rifles made good progress, scaling the slopes to the left of the Boer position, but the hapless Northumberlands, con-fronted by the intermittent cliff, either sought refuge in its lee from the fusillade or funnelled into the defiles, scrabbling upwards like dassies. Across the basin the blinded artillery began its bombardment, lobbing shrapnel onto the vanguard of the British assault. The advance faltered, then broke. Back fell the shaken Northumberlands, their colonel mortally wounded, and they streamed across the plain as the bullets spat around them. Gatacre, powerless to do otherwise, ordered the retreat. Back fell the disheartened Irish Rifles, having made steady progress but emasculated by the collapse. Some ran between me and the bakkie, stumbling, falling, while others huddled at the foot of the cliff, immobilised by fear and fatigue. Only the artillery held, continuing their bombardment, sending shells whistling over my head which burst dramatically above the Boer positions, keeping the burghers at bay as Gatacre's force fled in disarray, unwittingly, as you know, leaving a third of its number behind.

During all this a kwedin rode past on a bicycle, staring incredulously at an idiot in a chair apparently transfixed by an utterly unremarkable mountain. Away towards the Van Zyl homestead, where the slackers had slaughtered the pregnant ewes, a tractor advanced along a bumpy track with behind it a plough whose raised shears suggested the poised front legs of a praying mantis. As I loaded the chair and cooker into the bakkie, the tractor bounced past, its driver lifting a hand in greeting, and headed northwards around the Kissieberg and its sister koppies in the direction of the junction itself. To continue my last lap, as it were, I followed, soon reaching the trading post and siding. Deciding not to climb to the redoubts on the slopes of Rooikop, I parked not far from the store and took several photographs for later reference before merely sitting in the cab and surveying the surroundings. Among my imaginings was what everything had looked like to the young Winston Churchill when he passed through a month before the battle and witnessed the evacuation of the British garrison just prior to the Boer advance.

Ahead of me, across the district road, a large Friesland cow was resolutely polling a prickly pear bush. Stretching her neck between strands of barbed-wire, she nibbled at each succulent leaf, seemingly indifferent to its thorns, and then tore a chunk of the green flesh and chewed with apparent relish what I imagined to be as bitter as the aloe juice painted on my nails as a child to prevent me from biting them.

Just then Meiring the trader appeared amidst his Dobermans in the yard behind his house. Crossing to the fence, I reintroduced myself and explained the reason for my visit.

'Come,' he said, 'let me show you something I forgot to show you last time. It would be good for you to see it before you leave.'

'Thank you,' I replied, following him around his corrugated-iron bungalow to a blockhouse which reared among an effusion of prickly pear bushes not far from the district road.

Like everything else at that high altitude, it had weathered well, the precision of its masonry reminiscent of Daan Fourie's cottage at Fluistervlakte. Towering above us, with its solidity, height, raised doorway and ingeniously positioned turrets, it declared its invincibility with the boldness of a klaxon, but had never been put to the test. A previous owner had knocked another door through the stone at ground level and Meiring unlocked it and ushered me inside. Light, shot through with dust motes, shafted in through the loopholes, exposing the stark simplicity of the interior despite the tea chests brimming with bric-a-brac and a lawnmower and roll of polythene piping. Diametrically opposite each other were two latrines, and a wooden staircase rose diagonally up one wall and through the ceiling to the floor above. There I found the original entrance, its steel doors bolted, and a trapdoor above and below to facilitate the movement of ammunition boxes. Climbing another flight of stairs, we reached the top storey with its canopy of corrugated iron, unrestricted view and its twin steel turrets which protruded from opposite corners.

'Look,' said Meiring, leading me into one of the box-like protuberances and pointing through its loopholes, 'this covers those enemy who actually get to the walls. This one covers two sides and the other one the other two.'

So solid did the building appear that it seemed almost a pity that it had never been attacked. A successful defence would have justified the effort of its construction: the importation of probably everything except the stone, and its laborious transportation over hundreds of kilometres from the coast to this lost corner of the high hinterland.

I told this to Meiring who laughed. 'Don't be too sure that it won't see any action. Sometimes when I see the news on TV I think that it won't be long before I move in here. You heard about that Naas Roussouw? Things are getting bad now.'

'Yes,' I said, 'there's a lot of trouble.'

At the mention of Naas's name, I blanched but rallied promptly, my skillful separation of the sighting and the murder having strengthened my resilience. Meiring, obviously glad of company and encouraged by my enthusiastic response to the blockhouse, invited me for coffee which I declined only because it was already mid-morning and I had still to visit Montmorency's death place and his grave. Shaking hands vigorously, we wished each other well and I remember glimpsing as I pulled away the elderly trader and his entourage of Dobermans disappearing behind an outhouse while the ruminating cow looked on placidly.

Rising out of the basin, I crossed the neck at which Gatacre had initially aimed his attack and returned to Molteno along the Steynsberg road — the route of the British retreat — before branching off to pay my last respects to the hero of Omdurman.

Choosing to trespass rather than drive to the farmhouse and risk lengthy assurances about the military's ability to contain the insurrection, I parked on the verge and headed across country in what I assumed to be the correct direction. The going was heavy, the terrain rutted by erosion and studded with rocks, and it was noon before I found the cairn. As I had done several months previously, I scanned the surrounding veld to get my bearings, took a few photographs, whispered an incantation of sorts to give me luck with my writing and returned to the bakkie.

My next stop, at the Molteno cemetery, was shorter still, being merely a pause beside the brotherhood of tombstones, and another few photographs and another incantation. I

133

then had a light lunch at the Central Hotel before visiting the town museum. It was late afternoon when, with the last lap almost complete, I set out for Toomnek and home.

During the journey I listened on the radio to a programme of songs from the sixties. Among those played was Roy Orbison's 'Only the Lonely', that mawkish ballad which seemed then to touch the solitariness of my guilt. Even after the song had ended, its pitiful refrain kept echoing in my head and I gazed through the windscreen to its accompaniment.

A kilometre or so from Toomnek the road rises suddenly and then begins its gradual descent to the village, separating the precise greens and bunkers of the country club golf course from the sordid jumble of the black township. That evening, on reaching the crest to sixties accompaniment, I anticipated the usual display of streetlamps and glowing braziers but was confronted instead by quite another spectacle: the pulsating blue light of a police road-block, great wreaths of smoke and the reek of burning rubber.

Stopping, my apprehension strangely at odds with the effervescent music, I sat and waited. Presently a policeman approached, making his way down the row of winking brake-lights, and lowered his face at the window.

'Evening sir,' he said in Afrikaans. 'Where are you going to?'

'Skemerfontein. Mr Murray's farm on the Fluistervlakte road.'

'Thank you,' he nodded. 'You can go through.'

'What's the problem?' I asked, pointing at the smoke.

'There's a bit of trouble in the township. But the troops are sorting it out.'

As I edged past the police and their vehicles and began my descent, I glanced to my right and saw down one of the township's rutted streets a crowd of blacks mafficking around a pyramid of burning tyres. They were chanting and ululating, and the combined sound both frightened and exhilarated me. It was then that I noticed the convoy of Buffels turning off the tarmac and advancing awkwardly like stag beetles between the shanties. Their side flaps were up and only the troops' helmets and rifle muzzles bristled above the defences.

Caught within my convoy, I pressed on, imagining the probable sequence of the confrontation: loud-hailer, tear gas, rubber bullets, then lead. Cordoned by the police, anything could happen beyond the burning barricades while life elsewhere continued, unaware and unaffected. To all but the witnesses, the bloodshed would be a story, malleable in the hands of its tellers.

However, the police containment hadn't been complete. Beyond the pines which divided the township from the municipal cemetery I saw by the lights of another pyre of tyres a band of black youths advancing on the graves. Armed with what looked like metal pipes or fencing standards, they began smashing the tombstones, topping crosses and angels and pulverising vases, scattering their sad displays of flowers across the marble chips. Noticing the wanton destruction, an elderly white man in a car ahead of me hooted, shouting and gesticulating from his window. At this, one of the youths paused, brandishing his length of pipe defiantly and shouted something while I watched in horror, caressed by the gentleness of Scott McKenzie's 'San Francisco', the dull thuds of the blows punctuating the music like discordant drumming. With each blow so the ferocity of the attackers seemed to increase until they were felling memorials like cutters would fell stalks of cane. As we inched forward, bumper to bumper, I remember thinking that people would be killed that evening. The desecration of the graves would incense the troops.

Convinced of the accuracy of my hunch, I listened to the news on the radio both later that night and first thing in the morning, but there was no mention of unrest in Toomnek. A black constable had been fatally stabbed in Natal and two black children injured by police action in Soweto. Otherwise, the country had been peaceful over the preceding twenty-four hour period.

In Toomnek, rumours were rife. A caddie at the golf club said fourteen people had been shot dead by the troops while policemen questioned in the Royal Hotel bar by Hennie Lotter had emphatically denied the accusations. Nobody, they said, had been killed or injured. The crowd had dispersed peacefully after tear gas had been used and several warning shots fired. A few of the desecrators had been arrested and were awaiting trial. False rumours of fatalities were merely part of the strategy of destabilisation. The public shouldn't listen to them.

During my last few days at Skemerfontein I grilled myself about the desecrators. Having thrown in my lot with the struggle, did I support their action? My answer, although timorous, had conviction: No, but yes.

TWENTY

Like three crushing punches on the nose, with the resultant
splattering of blood, the defeats of Black Week stopped the
British Field Force in its tracks. An interlude of reassessment
followed, and the adoption of remedial measures: numerous
reinforcements were accumulated and Buller was superseded
by Lord Roberts, with Lord Kitchener as his Chief of Staff.
The same Kitchener, you will remember, whom we last
encountered weeping among the ruins of Khartoum and
taking as bounty the Mahdi's head before having second
thoughts and ordering its burial in the cemetery at Wadi
Halfa. And the same Kitchener, you will also remember,
who thought so highly of Gatacre.

Roberts's strategy was simple: to consolidate his forces,
follow the railway line from Cape Town to Kimberley, and
then march eastwards via Bloemfontein to Pretoria and
secure the branch lines to Durban and Lourenço Marques.

After reoccupying the vacated Stormberg Junction,
Gatacre's Third Division headed northwards to join the
main column, arriving at Bethulie just in time to prevent the
retreating Boers from blowing up the railway bridge across
the Orange River. Here, once again, the general's foolhardiness became apparent. Accompanied only by a Royal En-
gineers lieutenant, he himself crept along the parapet under
cover of darkness to cut free parcels of explosives attached
to the bridge. Not the behaviour of a general and divisional
commander, surely, but another loop of the same thread
which stitches brigand-hunting in the hills outside Quetta
to storming the zeriba at Atbara. Like a row of telephone
poles receding into the past, so examples of Gatacre's reckless-
ness seem to flank his progress.

On taking Bloemfontein, Roberts offered to pardon all
burghers who laid down their arms and swore allegiance to
Queen Victoria. Needing to disperse his troops throughout

the Orange Free State to facilitate the anticipated capitulation, he ordered detachments to various centres. Thus the British found themselves over a barrel, as it were, needing to be both omnipresent and invulnerable. With his troop numbers grossly inadequate for the task, Roberts found himself commanding a force spread so thinly over the veld that only extreme nimbleness could avert disaster. Consequently, whenever a detachment was threatened, Roberts had one of two options: to recall it speedily or to bolster it with reinforcements.

One such case occurred on March 30, 1900, when he ordered a detachment at Dewetsdorp to withdraw to the safety of Bloemfontein. En route, however, it was surrounded by Boers several kilometres to the east of Reddersburg. Gatacre was then ordered to march to its assistance, but the defenders — many of whom were veterans of the Stormberg debacle — surrendered just before his arrival. His alleged tardiness during his advance, and his failure to pursue the retreating Boers in an attempt to release the prisoners, convinced Roberts and Kitchener that Gatacre could no longer be relied upon for senior command.

Yet again, Winston Churchill was at the hub of history and it is to him that we must turn for a firsthand account of our protagonist's fall from grace. Stopping for the night at Bethany while en route for Bloemfontein, Churchill discovered the presence of Gatacre whom he had last met up the Nile. Eager to hear about the battle of Stormberg, the young correspondent sought out the general, finding him in a corrugated-iron house beside the railway line:

I thought him greatly altered from the dashing, energetic man I had known up the river, or had heard about on the frontier or in plague-stricken Bombay. Four months of anxiety and abuse had left their mark on him. The weary task of keeping things going with utterly insufficient resources, and in the face of an adroit and powerful enemy in a country where every advantage lay with the Boer, had bowed that iron frame and tired the strange energy which had made him so remarkable among soldiers. But when he thought of the future his face brightened. The dark days were over. He had his whole division at last. Moreover, there was prospect of immediate action. So I left him, for it was growing late. Early next morning he was dismissed from his command and ordered to England, broken, ruined and disgraced.

Within hours he was gone, arriving back in London a month later and shortly thereafter resuming his command of the Eastern District. Those early days of his eclipse must have been particularly difficult, especially when the tide turned in South Africa and he had to applaud the victories of a team from which he had just been dropped. But he constrained his bitterness and it is only from Beatrix that we get inklings of the vastness of his disappointment.

On the completion of his term of command in late 1903, Gatacre was partly put out to grass, as it were, being commissioned to update the lists of registered horses in twenty-two counties. This task he tackled with characteristic zest, revealing his unabated athleticism during a six-week stint at Salisbury when, rather than take the train home during weekends, he chose to cycle the sixty-four miles, a remarkable accomplishment for a man of sixty.

Despite his health and enthusiasm, however, his days in the military were numbered. Unable to cleanse himself of the taint of dismissal, he found his options steadily narrowing until in March 1905 he received notification that his services were no longer required. Deprived of his raison d'etre, he found himself suddenly adrift until a timely offer of a directorship in a certain Kordofan Trading Company with interests in rubber in Abyssinia provided substitute grist for his restlessness.

Several months later he was offered a trip to the company's rubber forests near Addis Ababa and accepted with alacrity, immersing himself in the intricacies of the rubber trade and making detailed preparations. Selfless yet again, or perhaps merely pragmatic, devoted Beatrix was delighted for her husband and gave the expedition her blessing.

Leading a party including a Syrian trader who had been

his interpreter in Egypt seven years previously, Gatacre set off up the White Nile, passing Omdurman and Khartoum, before branching eastwards up a tributary to Gambela and thence three hundred miles across land to Addis Ababa.

How his spirits must have lifted as he breathed the heat and dust, his lean frame taut with exhilaration, his thoughts far from the responses of pity and the *schadenfreude* that he had come to associate with England.

When the expedition's three boats ran aground before Gambela, it was Gatacre himself who continued on foot and arranged for several hundred porters to lug the merchandise to Addis Ababa. But on his return journey to the river the end came suddenly and rather tamely for a man who had risked his life so often. Bivouacking one evening in a swamp, he caught a fever from which he died, on January 18, 1906. His retainers transported his body by canoe to Gambela where he was buried in the Abyssinian Christian Cemetery. And there his remains lie, apparently beneath a tombstone which pathetically lists all his accomplishments as if to implore passers-by not to forget his illustrious past before he took a chance and failed.

Being one of the world's polecats, I will never see his grave. There can be few things more certain than that the Ethiopians won't grant me entry into their country. As a white South African I have learnt to limit my mobility to land south of the Limpopo, excluding the occasional excursion to Namibia, Botswana or Zimbabwe. Until Elias Mbuyembu and his comrades return in triumph and the dance of liberation sanitises me as an African, I must be content with this southern tip of the continent. As for Gatacre's resting place, I have to rely on historical sources and my imagination.

TWENTY-ONE

On the day I left Skemerfontein it was raining. After a downpour the previous night, a steady drizzle was falling, caressing the corrugated-iron roofs and murmuring down the drainpipes. Having packed the bakkie the previous day and sent several boxes on ahead by train, I paid off Hester, thanking her and wishing her well. Then I walked through the cottage for the last time, saying goodbye to it with a strange mixture of melancholy and relief.

It was about eight when I drove slowly down the hillside, keeping astride the pronounced middlemannetjie to prevent the bakkie from slewing in the stickiness. Having had dinner with Angus and Mary the previous evening, and said goodbye to them then, I didn't stop at the main house but drove on past the sheds, silo and crushpen, accelerating slightly when I reached the driveway with its harsh all-weather surface.

As I began the gradual descent to the gate with its cattle-grid and merino ram sign, I glanced in parting in the rearview mirror and saw Angus standing in the vegetable garden in the rain. With his slouch hat and bulky raincoat, he triggered a vivid image from my childhood: a scarecrow in a tattered trench coat which teetered like a drunk within a dell of pawpaws, appearing to remonstrate with the marauding bands of mousebirds that pecked neat tunnels in the salmon-coloured fruit. Momentarily, before rounding the gentle curve beside the prickly pears and the disused reservoir, I saw Angus raise his arm in farewell, and then he was gone, veiled by the cedars and the rain pattering on the misting glass.

Not far from the Skemerfontein gate I entered the dip in the district road where Naas had encountered Gatacre amidst the milling sheep and I had seen Elias Mbuyembu dart down the adjoining sloot. The association of murderer and victim sent my thoughts back down that well-trodden track through culpability, doubt and acceptance to a recollection of Naas's funeral in the Dutch Reformed church in Toomnek several weeks before. Seated at the back beside Mary, Angus and the Thorntons, I remember fearing revelation by an omniscient god, imagining a stentorian voice reproaching me in Afrikaans and the entire congregation swivelling and staring. But of course nothing happened; tellingly, perhaps.

The feeling of solidarity among the large white congregation was almost tangible, and I remember marvelling at how effortlessly the mourners had subverted their differences, becoming merely whites in Africa for a cathartic hour of fellowship and grief. Although the police and other essential services retained skeleton staffs, most shops were closed while their owners attended the service. Consequently, the village was devoid of whites and the pavements were thronged with blacks who mooched and nattered as the bell tolled and the sound of dirges welled from the cool interior into the dusty heat.

But it was after the service that I reached my nadir. I was waiting beside Mary and Angus as they exchanged pleasantries with members of the dispersing congregation when I found myself confronted by Koos and Oom Piet. Clearly distraught and supported by friends, they were being helped to a car when our eyes met and I mumbled a few words of condolence. It was Koos who replied: 'Thank you Jerry,' he said in Afrikaans. 'Naas was very fond of you.'

Reaching the T-junction some eight kilometres from Toomnek, I turned left, away from my familiar route, and headed for Natal and home. At first the road was cambered tarmac scything through ordered farms sprinkled with windmills and sheep until the Transkeian border heralded potholes and goats and a surrounding patchwork of subsistence plots ribbed with erosion. With my attention half on the road and half back at Skemerfontein, I mulled over the preceding year as I sped homewards, linking disparate images as a swallowtail links flowers on its lilting path: the wrinkled snouts of bleating sheep; Angus, surrounded by books, cleaning his shotgun; the sighing of the pines behind my cottage; naked Martie basked in coloured lights; the photograph of Gatacre on the frontispiece of Beatrix's apologia; the soldiers' shattered memorial among the poplars; and blood splatters on the linoleum beside Naas's body.

But most of all I thought of Katie and how meeting her had made all the difference. As I sped along, I recalled the good times we had spent together at Skemerfontein, focusing on scenes of quiet domesticity — reading together, eating together, bathing together, loving together — before my thoughts moved on and saw us on the lawn, in the pines and meandering over the mountaintop. Focusing more closely I found us lying naked on my bed one balmy afternoon as several insects buzzed bouncingly across a window pane and water tinkled from the windmill pipe into the reservoir. In that interlude of peacefulness that follows lovemaking, we were both reading, Katie immersed in Sartre's *Intimacy* and myself in Churchill's *River War*. And in the suggestions of abandonment, the calm community of our postures, and the separateness of our reading, I saw the strength of our relationship. Together, I knew we were indomitable.

As I dropped from the escarpment to the lowlands, so I felt my guilt begin to recede. Leaving the scene of one's crime far behind has a marvellously therapeutic effect. With the gradual emergence of the coastal luxuriance and humidity, the actual existence of the Roussouws' arid gully with its little cottage began to seem improbable. Perhaps Gatacre had felt a similar rejuvenation when he headed for the depths of Abyssinia. There, on a new venture in north-eastern Africa, even the Stormberg must have seemed galaxies away.

When I reached the sea and headed northwards, with long lines of breakers curling several hundred metres to my right, I felt my spirits begin to rise. In the blueness of the water with its white fissures, the waxen greenness of the flanking bush and the molten glare of the coastal sunlight, I felt myself embrace all that I have often detested. Winding down the window, I let the humidity slap me in the face and rejoiced in its cloyingness. This, I told myself, is where I belong. Despite the oppressively damp heat, the mambas and the mosquitoes, I knew then that I needed the sound of the sea, the call of the black-collared barbet and the moaning of bamboos in the night. Unlike the loneliness of the Stormberg's high quietness, the subtropical effusiveness was as much a part of me as my Mbuyembu secret.

Not far south of Durban I came across an accident. Two cars travelling in the same direction had somehow collided and one was in the gutter while the other was half concealed in an adjoining field of sugar cane. Amongst the glass strewn over the tarmac were a police van and an ambulance whose red light pulsed slowly. With all the police and ambulance men attempting to extract someone from the car in the cane, a bystander had filled the breach and was guiding the traffic through the bottleneck. He was a portly man, dressed in khakis like a farmer, and as cars slowed and eased into the single lane to avoid the wreckage and a corpse covered in a grey blanket, he waved them through with a cheerfulness that was both incongruous and strangely affirmative. Coming home with a welt of guilt across my memories of the previous year, I was in need of some sign of forgiveness which that ruddy-faced police substitute could be made to provide. Within feet of the corpse, his smile and wave as he ushered each car through the narrows seemed dismissive of violent death and supportive of life. As I passed him, I felt my guilt become history. That it would always be with me I knew, but it had finally joined the past, and the future lay ahead.

While such a speedy exorcism may appear a little cosy, I had wilfully conjured in the gestures of that surrogate traffic policeman the symbols of my absolvement. Like Gatacre in Abyssinia, I was back on course and the corpse beneath the grey blanket, Naas Roussouw in the Toomnek cemetery and the Tommies buried in the lee of the Kissieberg were merely unfortunate instances of Fate's capriciousness. Exhilarated, I turned on the radio and to a reggae rhythm gunned through the fields of arrowing cane.

Reaching the periphery of Durban, I arced leftwards, taking the ring road which skirts the city to the west. Signs on the highway announced the routes to several black townships, each tucked out of sight in the folds in the rolling hills. At the KwaMashu offramp, I saw a column of smoke curling in the near distance and knew immediately from my stints there as a national serviceman that its source was burning

144

rubber. I could picture the scene: a pyramid of tyres engulfed in flames, a gathering crowd and the steady advance of Buffels brimming with troops.

From the occupants of passing cars it appeared that the private schools had just broken up for the Christmas holidays. Sleek saloons with their boots heavy with trunks and sporting equipment swept past me towards the north coast and Zulu-land. Exuberant teenage faces bobbed in the back seats while groomed fathers steered effortlessly and svelte mothers swivelled, nattering and offering snacks. As they passed me I wondered if anyone in those plush interiors had noticed the smoke. And if they had, did they have any inkling of its origin? Probably not. But like the schoolchildren, I was homeward bound, and with the beginnings of *Dignity in Defeat* beside me and the knowledge that Katie would be arriving soon, I was also too excited for gloomy realities. It was like the Toomnek township incidents and countless others country-wide: a flare-up discreetly quashed while life continues seemingly unaffected.

With Billy Ocean bursting from the radio, I filtered off the highway and headed down a wide dirt road towards the sea. A tractor towing a trailer laden with cane passed in the opposite direction and through the dispersing dust I saw across the expanse of cane the familiar knoll poised, sphinx-like, above the beach. Next I glimpsed the roof, then flashes of garden, before reaching the long driveway that meandered beneath a canopy of branches to the cottage.

After stopping on the pinkish gravel between the kitchen and the garage, I sat briefly in the cab with the music play-ing and absorbed the familiar surroundings: the cool white-ness of the walls, the deep verandah buttressed with bougain-villaea, and the sea beyond with its swell sheened by the afternoon light. All appeared as it should be. By then another song was playing on the radio, something soft and sweeping. To its accompaniment I stepped out of the bakkie, imagining myself falling to my knees and kissing the soil like a returning exile. As I walked across the lawn to where the terrace fell away sharply towards the beach, so the sound of the song faded until it became the sound of the sea.

EPILOGUE

Now that I have just finished this account of my year at Skemerfontein, I think I will call it *The Desecration of the Graves*, for obvious reasons. As yet I have had no definite offers for the Gatacre biography, but several publishers have expressed interest and tell me that they will be making a decision soon. These things take time, I know, and I am prepared to wait. And now that this laatlammetjie has been born, I may even submit it for publication, although a certain amount of fudging will be necessary. Anyway, it's too early to tell. With so much in flux at the moment, it's impossible to be specific. And I'd like to keep my options open.

Not long after my return to Natal, Katie joined me, having been granted permission by the university authorities to complete her Master's here. She has commandeered one of the spare-rooms which is now cluttered with her paraphernalia and smells pleasantly of raw turpentine. Among the easel, tubes of paint and quiver of brushes are the Fluistervlakte photographs from which she works, and it is strangely reassuring now to see Daan Fourie, Hendrik and Santie Vosloo, and Anna Strydom, if not for themselves then for the memories that Katie and I share of that outing.

Although it took much soul-searching, I have told Katie about the Elias Mbuyembu incident. Initially I had great reservations about revealing my secret but weakened as our relationship developed and withholding it began to seem more and more deceitful. Luckily, she took it well, saying that she would have done the same under the circumstances. We have sworn ourselves to secrecy so what you read may differ slightly from the truth or, alternatively, may not, the assumption being that you think it does. And so, you see, I can tell the truth under the guise of fiction, or fictionalise with the supposed credibility of fact, or both. It's all very ingenious, I think.

The Jeremy Cranwell before Skemerfontein was very different from the person who is writing this. I told you that in the prologue and stand by it now more than ever. During that year when I ticked to the slow tempo of the farm, sounding the past and being confronted by the present, I was pushed off the fence, as it were, and forced to take a stand. Since then, I must confess, I have in moments of weakness contemplated parting the strands and crossing over, but barbs of doubt have always been a deterrent. Forcing me to hesitate and reconsider, they can be credited as much as my resolve for my present determination to look only to the future. Fear is a powerful bogey which must be contained; otherwise one flounders and all is lost. When I peer at the fearful through the strands as they follow their leaders as blindly as sheep, I am sad for them because their fears will be realised. Only by mastering their anxiety can they defeat it. And that is what I have tried to do.

Katie, of course, has always been a ballast. At each upsurge of my guilt she is quick in support. She has made it her business to ensure my well-being and, like Beatrix, she is as attentive as a devotee although it is I who am indebted. We are to have another celebration tonight, just a simple affair as we had several months ago to wish the biography copies well on their journeys. Small as it is, *The Desecration of the Graves* deserves a launch as it may even become my flagship if nothing becomes of Gatacre. As before, Katie and I will settle on the verandah in our wicker chairs while the sun descends into the cane, appearing to puncture itself on the arrowed tips of the stalks. After the customary toasts, we will drink and natter as the waves tumble and rush and the bats zigzag through the shadows with the fever of guilty thoughts. Beside us, on a table, a mosquito coil will smoulder, its glowing tip spiralling inexorably towards the centre. And with the drink we will laugh and reminisce about Skemerfontein like friends remembering a mutual lover long deceased.

Only the death of the Indian fisherman will dampen our merriment. Swept off the rocks yesterday while gaffing a hammerhead, he hasn't yet been found. Rescue boats have searched, but without success. Police divers have probed among the crayfish crevices but have also returned empty-handed. While I didn't know the man, I had grown accustomed to his slight, bow-legged frame scuttling along the waterline with a long rod soaring from his shoulder. It was he who announced several months ago that he wanted to talk to me. Although he never appeared, he frequently waylaid Katie during her beach excursions and plied her with crayfish and shad. With each insistent offering we became more alarmed, fearing a favour that required such softening. But now we will never know. His niggling anxiety will remain a secret.

Even if neither book is published, my father's legacy will keep Katie and me going. We have resolved to live as simply as possible, both plugging away at our chosen crafts. A society so rich in trauma is a marvellous creative source and my brush with the struggle has ensured that I am connected. With each news item on further violence, I seethe with idealism and guilt and reach for my pen. Hoping to become two latter-day Thoreaus, with this corner of the Indian Ocean for our Walden Pond, we will till our vegetable garden behind the cottage and, like strandlopers, comb the rock pools for mussels. There is nothing particularly novel in this choice; it is necessary to ensure a lifetime's private income amidst a destroyed economy, and in its simplicity avoids the grossness of ostentation in a society in which poverty is rife. It will be our token to egalitarianism; not much, perhaps, but it will ease the consciences of two privileged white South Africans who are committed to the future.

And I must learn to accept that I may have murdered Naas, vicariously, that is. You know that my intentions were honourable and I wished nobody harm. Compassion was my only motive. But, like Gatacre, I mustn't whinge. I must press on, not deep into the heart of Ethiopia but into this stretch of African coastline where I belong. I must come to really know the place, as I tried at Skemerfontein: to know its seasons, the fauna and flora, its different inhabitants, in fact everything about this band of bush sandwiched between the cane fields and the sea. There must be no more transience. As Euro-Africans with a shotgun in the cupboard, Katie and I will keep to ourselves as the combatants wrestle for supremacy.

On the slope behind our cottage, set deep in the bush a hundred metres from the kitchen door, is a clearing boxed by large fig trees. In its centre are three mounds which Katie and I assume to be graves. Who the occupants are and how long they have been there is anyone's guess, but the lie of the undergrowth and the mounds themselves suggest antiquity. As part of our resolution to assimilate ourselves, Katie and I hope to be buried there. Despite the probability of a law prohibiting something so unorthodox, we will persevere in the hope that one day we too will rest in that peaceful setting. Whether or not to have tombstones, however, is a dilemma. While there is something to be said for a record of one's existence, there may also come a time in this country when the mere sight of a European surname on a grave may invite desecration. Do we rest incognito or declare our presence? As yet we are unsure.

Late last night when we broke for tea before bed, Katie produced a quotation which she felt fitted Gatacre perfectly. Attributed to La Bruyere, the seventeenth century moralist, it went thus: 'Men fall from great fortune because of the same shortcomings that lead to their rise.' At first I was slow on the uptake, being transfixed by a leaf fragment which rotated slowly in my cup like the tip of a mosquito coil, but she prompted me with the single word that I already knew: restlessness. It was that same strange disquiet and inexhaustibility, she said, which had propelled Gatacre up the ranks and ensured his eventual fall from grace. Without it, he would have been both less spectacular and less vulnerable, but he had it, and that was that. Success and failure were Gatacre's lot. But what made him different from many others who failed was that his fires weren't soused by his fall. Instead, after a spell of benumbment, his dynamo resumed its nagging motion, propelling him along a different tack. Had not the miasmas of that Abyssinian swamp got him, there is every chance that he may have transformed his failure into a success of sorts. Had he died in his club

149

while playing billiards, or in an armchair in his study, he would have been merely one of many others. But that he set out aged sixty-two for darkest Africa, the continent that had witnessed both his success and failure, made him vastly different from those who chose comfortable retirement among commiserating colleagues. For all his limitations, Gatacre was an original. And that's what makes his story worth exhuming.

My historical-literary pretensions are similarly loaded with success or failure. But, like Gatacre, I plan to meet the furies head on and am determined to endure. If *Dignity in Defeat* never becomes typescript, I will submit *The Desecration of the Graves* for publication, and should that also fail, I will seek another subject to embalm. Perhaps Katie and my life-style here has literary potential. I could try and write a novel about a young white couple living in a cottage encircled by coastal bush during a period of political volatility and transition. I could introduce, under cover of darkness, several black saboteurs seeking refuge after a mission in a nearby city. By juxtaposing both sets of characters I could emphasise the white couple's quandary: whether or not to assist in the birth of an order that promises equality but threatens to erase Europeanism. That, being the essence of white South Africa's fears, is fertile soil in which an assortment of narratives can be made to grow. So, you see, no matter which of my works fail, there will always be others. Should failure stare me in the face, I intend to do as Gatacre did and press on.

Since I shared my secret with Katie, she has begun another painting. Both similar and dissimilar to her Fluistervlakte portraits, it is a head and shoulders of Naas. Unlike the weathered realism of the Fouries, Vosloos and Strydoms, with their burnt sienna faces and dunnish clothing, this new venture has a blunt grotesqueness reminiscent of Francis Bacon's work. While the likeness to Naas is not readily apparent among the simian distortions, closer observation reveals a prominent nose and loose lower lip beneath which she has stroked a slash of silver. To the unknowing, the stripe could be a reflection or a laser of sunlight, but to us it is the sheen of saliva which forever shone like snail-wake across the stubble on his chin. Whether or not Katie will hang this painting with her Fluistervlakte collection, she has yet to decide, but should it gain the approval of her examiner, it will for the two of us give her exhibition a certain pathos while also forming a surreal counterpoint to the realism of her other works. As the second, smaller panel of a diptych, as it were, her Naas painting could be suggestive of the Afrikaners' psyche, that secret part which quavers behind their rough-hewn intractability. For us, of course, it will also be a memorial to a friend who was caught in the cross-fire.

From my desk, where I am writing this, I have a panoramic view of both our garden and the sea. Through the sprays of bougainvillaea slung low beneath the pergola, I can see the breakers as they slide shorewards, their wavering lines like white streamers in a slow wind tunnel. To the north, a knoll of milkwoods intrudes, shortening the perspective, forcing one's vision inwards along a crescent of azaleas to where the gravel driveway meanders up a hillside canopied with flat-crowns. As I gaze at the dapples beneath the branches, the Indian postman emerges, cycling down the road with his white topi tailed by a bulging haversack. Dismounting at the gate, he inserts a wad of envelopes into the letter-box.

Whenever I witness him making his delivery, I am filled with apprehension, telling myself that among those envelopes could be a real acceptance. While watching him just now, the indicators seemed good, my inner voice dancing with optimism. As soon as I'm finished this I'll go out and see. If the news is good, I'll yell across the dunes to Katie and she'll yelp joyously and hurry for home. While she weaves up between the amatungulus and wild bananas, I'll luxuriate in the knowledge that Gatacre has been resurrected at last.

When I look up the postman has gone, only the whiteness of his topi bobbing briefly within the canopy until it is enveloped by the dapples. I must end now and discover what tidings he has brought. Even if the odds are stacked against me, I must find out.

151

BIBLIOGRAPHY

Amery, L.S. (ed.). *The Times History of the War in South Africa 1899–1902* (London 1907).

Aucamp, Hennie, (ed.) *Op die Stormberge: 'n Vertolking van 'n Streek* (Cape Town and Johannesburg 1971).

Breytenbach, J.H. *Die Geskiedenis van die Tweede Vryheidsoorlog 1899–1902*. vol.2 (Pretoria 1971).

Churchill, W.S. *Ian Hamilton's March* (London 1900).

Churchill, W.S. *London to Ladysmith* (London 1900).

Churchill, W.S. *The River War* (London 1899).

Conan Doyle, A. *The Great Boer War* (London 1902).

Creswicke, L. *South Africa and the Transvaal War,* 6 volumes (Edinburgh 1901).

Danes, R. *Cassell's History of the Boer War 1899–1901* (London 1901).

Davitt, M. *The Boer Fight for Freedom* (New York 1902).

Farwell, B. *The Great Boer War* (London 1976).

Gardner, B. *The African Dream* (London 1970).

Gatacre, B. *The Story of the Life and Services of Sir William Forbes Gatacre* (London 1910).

Kruger, D.W. *Dictionary of South African Biography,* vol.2 (Cape Town and Johannesburg 1972).

Kruger, R. *Good-bye Dolly Gray: The Story of the Boer War* (London 1964).

Meintjies, J. *Stormberg: A Lost Opportunity* (Cape Town 1969).

Montgomery-Massingberd, H. (ed.) *Burke's Landed Gentry,* vol.3 (London 1972).

Pakenham, T. *The Boer War* (London 1979).

Steevens, G.W. *From Cape Town to Ladysmith* (Edinburgh and London 1900).

Steevens, G.W. *With Kitchener to Khartoum* (London 1898).

Warner, P. *Kitchener: The Man Behind the Legend* (London 1985).

Warwick, P. (ed.). *The South African War: The Anglo-Boer War 1899—1902* (Harlow 1980).

Wilson, H.W. *With the Flag to Pretoria,* 2 volumes (London 1900).

Van Wyk Smith, M. *Drummer Hodge: The Poetry of the Anglo-Boer War 1899—1902* (Oxford 1978).

Ziegler, P. *Omdurman* (London 1973).

GLOSSARY

amatungulu: evergreen shrub with waxy leaves and red fruit (from Zulu *amathungulu*)

baas: boss, master (Afrikaans)

bakkie: light truck, pick-up (Afrikaans)

besembos: any of several Karoo shrubs from which brooms are made (Afrikaans)

Boer: republican soldier in the Anglo-Boer War (Afrikaans)

boer: farmer (Afrikaans)

boerbul: South African dog bred mainly from the mastiff (Afrikaans)

boss boy: African man in charge of a group of workers

braai: to grill outdoors over the embers of a fire (Afrikaans)

Buffel: mine-proofed armoured vehicle (Afrikaans: buffalo)

burgher: citizen, usually of one of the Boer republics (Afrikaans)

bywoner: tenant farmer, poor white (Afrikaans)

cane: sugar cane, cane spirit

dassie: rock hyrax (Afrikaans)

DB: detention barracks

dominee: minister of the Dutch Reformed Church (Afrikaans) *doodgaan*: to die (Afrikaans)

doppie: empty cartridge case (Afrikaans)

Engelsman: Englishman (Afrikaans)

flat-crown: indigenous tree whose canopy has a flat, spreading crown

hamel: castrated sheep (Afrikaans)

harpuisbos: resin-secreting shrub found in the Karoo and environs (Afrikaans)

khaki: Boer name for a British soldier during the Anglo-Boer War

khakibos: noxious weed, the seed of which was brought to South Africa in fodder imported from South America by the British during the Anglo-Boer War (Afrikaans)

koppie, kopje: hillock (Afrikaans)

korhaan: bustard (Afrikaans)

kraal: enclosure for farm animals, or a cluster of huts (Afrikaans)

krantz: cliff (Afrikaans)

kriebos: spiny shrub common in the Stormberg (Afrikaans)

kwedin: young boy (Xhosa)

laatlammetjie: child born long after its siblings (Afrikaans)

land: cultivated or arable field (Afrikaans)

meerkat: suricate, small South African mammal resembling

a mongoose (Afrikaans)

middlemannetjie: continuous hump between wheel ruts on a dirt track (Afrikaans)

moer: to murder, beat up (Afrikaans)

mopani: common tree or shrub in low rainfall areas (from Setswana *mopane*)

platteland dorp: country town or village (Afrikaans)

push beat: do guard duty

R1: South African service rifle

rhebuck: small South African antelope (from Afrikaans *rhebok*)

rinkhals: Spitting Cobra or Ring-necked Cobra (Afrikaans)

rondavel: circular hut with conical roof

rooibos: bush tea thought to have medicinal properties (Afrikaans)

rooikat: lynx, caracal (Afrikaans)

sloot: ditch or small watercourse (Afrikaans)

stoep: covered verandah or open porch (Afrikaans)

strandloper: prehistoric coastal race of South Africa, possible forerunner of both the Bushman and Hottentot (Afrikaans)

strop: leather strap (Afrikaans)

umdoni: indigenous tree usually found near water (Zulu)

velskoen, veldskoen: any type of rough suede ankle-boot or shoe (Afrikaans)

verligte: enlightened, broadminded (Afrikaans)

volk: the people, usually the Afrikaner people

voorkamer: front room (Afrikaans)

zeriba: stockade or enclosure of thorn bushes (Arabic)